North Kingstown Library
100 Boone Street
North Kingstown, RI  02852
(401) 294-3306

# THE
# FAN-MAKER'S
# INQUISITION

# THE
# FAN-MAKER'S
# INQUISITION

*A Novel of the Marquis de Sade*

RIKKI DUCORNET

Henry Holt and Company | New York

Henry Holt and Company, LLC
*Publishers since 1866*
115 West 18th Street
New York, New York 10011

Portions of *The Fan-Maker's Inquisition*
were published in *Conjunctions.*

Library of Congress Cataloging-in-Publication Data
Ducornet, Rikki, 1943–
The fan-maker's inquisition : a novel of the marquis de Sade /
Rikki Ducornet.—1st ed.
p.     cm.
"Portions of The fan-maker's inquisition
were published in Conjunctions"—T.p. verso.
ISBN 0-8050-5926-1 (alk. paper)
1. France—History—Revolution, 1789–1799—Fiction.   2. Indians,
Treatment of—Mexico—Yucatán (State)—Fiction.   3. Sade, marquis de,
1740–1814—Fiction.   4. Landa, Diego de, 1524–1579—Fiction.
I. Title.
PS3554.U279F36    1999                                    99-10246
813'.54—dc21                                                 CIP

Henry Holt books are available for special promotions and
premiums. For details contact: Director, Special Markets.

First Edition 1999

Designed by Kelly S. Too

Printed in the United States of America
All first editions are printed on acid-free paper. ∞
1   3   5   7   9   10   8   6   4   2

In memory of my father,
who trusted me with *Justine;*
I was sixteen.

To Virgil, in friendship;
to Jonathan, to *plaisance.*

Sections of this novel were first published in *Conjunctions.* The author wishes to extend her thanks to Bradford Morrow, Tracy Brown, Sandra Dijkstra; to Guy, for the de Gouges library; to tireless, gentle Cath.

# THE
# FAN-MAKER'S
# INQUISITION

*Part* I

---

# THE
# FAN-MAKER'S
# INQUISITION

*There is no explosion except a book.*

*—Mallarmé*

ᗤ

# O N E

— A fan is like the thighs of a woman: It opens and closes. A good fan opens with a flick of the wrist. It produces its own weather—a breeze not so strong as to muss the hair.

There is a vocabulary attendant upon fan-making. Like a person, the fan has three principal parts: *Les brins,* or ribs, are most often of wood; *les panaches,* or, as courtesans call them, the legs, are also made of wood, or ivory, or mother-of-pearl (and these may also be jade: green—the color of the eye; rose—the color of the flesh; and white—the color of the teeth); the mount—and this is also a sexual term—which is sometimes called *la feuille,* or the leaf (another sexual term, dating, it is said, from the time of Adam)—the mount is made of paper, or silk, or swanskin—

— Swanskin?

— A fine parchment made from the skin of an unborn lamb, limed, scraped very thin, and smoothed down with pumice and chalk. The mount may be made of taffeta, or lace, or even feathers—but these are cumbersome. A fan trimmed with down has a tendency to catch to the lips if they are moist or rouged. A paper fan can be a treasure, especially if it is from Japan. The Japanese make the finest paper fans, and the most obscene. These are sturdier than one might think. Such a fan is useful when one is bored, forced to sup with an ailing relative whose ivory dentures stink. It is said that the pleated fan is an invention of the Japanese and that the Chinese collapsed in laughter when it was first introduced to China. The prostitutes, however, took to it at once.

— Why is that?

— Because it can be folded and tucked up a sleeve when, having lifted one's skirts and legs, one goes about one's business. Soon the gentlemen were sticking theirs down their boots—a gesture of evident sexual significance. Once I saw a fan from India: The *panaches* were carved to look like hooded cobras about to strike the naked beauty who, stretched out across the mount, lay sleeping. That was a beautiful fan.

— Earlier you referred to the three parts of the person. Name these.

— The head, the trunk, and the limbs.

— Exactly so. Please continue.

— Little mirrors may be glued to the fan so that one may admire oneself and dazzle others. It may be pierced with windows of mica or studded with gems. A telescopic lens may be attached to the summit of a *panache;* such a fan is useful at the theater. The Comtesse Gimblette owns a fan made of a solid piece of silver cut in the form of a heart and engraved with poetry:

> *Everything*
> Is to your taste.
> You snap up the world
> With haste!

A red fan is a symbol of love; a black one, of death, of course.

— When the fan in question—the one found in the locked chamber at La Coste—was ordered, what did Sade say, exactly?

— He came into the *atelier* looking very dapper, and he said: "I want to order a pornographic *ventilabrum*!" And he burst out laughing. I said: "I understand 'pornographic,' *monsieur,* but '*ventilabrum*'?" "A *flabellum*!" he cried, laughing even more. "With a scene of flagellation." "I can paint it on a *fan,*" I said, somewhat out of patience with him, although I have to admit I found him perfectly charming, "on velvet or on velum, and I can do you a *vernis Martin*—" This caused him to double over with hilarity. "Do me!" he cried. "*Do* me, you seductive, adorable fan-maker, a *vernis Martin* as best you can and as quickly as you can, and I will be your eternal servant." "You do me too much honor," I replied. Then I took down his order and asked for an advance to buy the ivory. (Because of the guild regulations, I purchase the skeletons from another craftsman.) Sade wanted a swanskin mount set to ivory— which he wanted *very* fine.

— Meaning?

— The ivory of domesticated elephants is brittle because the animals eat too much salt. Wild ivory is denser, far more beautiful and more expensive, too. For pierced work it cannot be surpassed. Then the mount needed thin slices of ivory cut into ovals for the faces, *les fesses,* the breasts . . .

— This request was unusual?

— I have received stranger requests, citizen.

— Continue.

— The slivers of ivory, no bigger than a fingernail, give beauty and interest to swanskin and velum—as does mother-of-pearl. I am sometimes able to procure these decorative elements for a fair price from a maker of buttons and belt buckles because I have an arrangement with him.

— Describe this arrangement.

— I paint his buttons.

— Continue.

— The making of buckles and buttons is not wasteful; nonetheless, there is always something left over, no matter the industry. I also use scraps to embellish the *panaches*—not where the fingers hold the fan, because over time the skin's heat causes even the best paste to soften. But farther up, the pieces hold so fast no one has ever complained.

— And this is the paste that was used to fix the six wafers to the upper section of the . . . mount?

— The same. Although I diluted it, as the wafers were so fragile.

— The entire fan is fragile.

— So I told Sade. He said it did not matter. The fan was an amusement. A gift for a whore.

— Some would call it blasphemy. Painting licentious acts, including sodomy, on the body of Christ.

— We are no more living beneath the boot of the Catholic Church, citizen. I never was a practicing Catholic. Like the paste that holds them to the fan, the wafers are made of flour and water. They are of human manufacture, and nothing can convince me of their sacredness.

— Your association with a notorious libertine and public enemy is under question today. Personally, I don't give a fig for blasphemy, although I believe there is no place in the Revolution for sodomites. But now, before we waste any more time, will you describe for the Comité the scenes painted on the fan. [The fan, in possession of the Comité de Surveillance de la Commune de Paris, is handed to her.] Is this the fan you made for Sade?

— Of course it is. [She examines the fan, briefly.] It is a convention to paint figures and scenes within cartouches placed against a plain background or, perhaps, a background decorated with a discreet pattern of stars, or hearts, or even eyes—as I have done here. In this case there are two sets of cartouches: the six painted wafers, well varnished, at the top, and the three large, isolated scenes beneath—three being the classic number.

— And now describe for the Comité the scenes.

— There is a spaniel.

— The girl is naked.

— All the girls are naked, as are all the gentlemen. Except for the Peeping Tom hiding just outside the window.

— And the spaniel.

— He is dressed in a little vest, and he carries a whip in his teeth.

— His master's whip?

— His master's whip.

— And the . . . master is in the picture, too?

— Yes! Smack in the middle. It is a portrait of Sade with an enormous erection!

— As specified in the agreement?

— Exactly. "Have it point to the *right!*" he said. "Because if I could fuck God right in the eye, I would." And he laughed. "Point it right for Hell," he said. So I did.

— The Comité is curious to know about your continued service to the Marquis de Sade.

— I paint pictures for him, and I—

— What is the nature of these pictures? Why is he wanting pictures?

— Because he is in prison! He has nothing before his eyes but the guillotine! All day he has nothing to occupy his mind but executions, and all night nothing but his own thoughts.

— Explosive thoughts.

—Yes. Those are his words: "explosive thoughts." He has told me that the pictures serve not only to amuse and occupy his mind. They also enable him to follow the itinerary of his madness—for he believes he is going mad and has little else to do but be the observer of his own destruction. "My head," he told me, "will be rolling soon." He was *not* referring to the guillotine. "If I didn't have your pictures," he said not long ago, "my skull would explode under the pressure of my imagination, and this tower splattered with blood and brains."

— Do you believe such a thing possible?

— Of course not. The walls splattered with blood and brains is a description of how he feels. He also says his head is an oven, an oven so hot it burns everything that goes into it. He says, "My daydreams are all char and smoke. The stench of my own thoughts makes it impossible to breathe."

— At this point, I would ask you to read aloud this letter—the first of many—taken from your rooms on the night of the eleventh.

— [Taking up the letter:] Ah! The one I call "A Cup of Chocolate."

*Little wolf, my prize wench. The things you sent have at last arrived this morning, pawed over by the contemptible Scrutinizer, a wretch who cannot keep his hands to himself; but nothing is broken and it seems that everything is in place:*

the ink, candles, linens, sugar, chocolate—the chocolate! Untouched! And what chocolate! So that I may start the day just as the Maya kings, with a foaming cup.

Like a good fuck, a good cup of chocolate starts with a vigorous whipping, and here I am, my little anis de Flavigny, breathing the Yucatán as I write this letter. There are fops who swear by ambergris and would put that in their chocolate, but I'm particular to the classic cup—unadulterated—perhaps the one instance when I can say I prefer a thing unadulterated!

A cup of chocolate, ma douce amie, and my mood—and it couldn't have been worse—has lifted; why, I am so buoyant that did God exist I'd be in Paradise with my nose up his arse! But this is a godless universe—you know it as well as I—and therefore nothing in the world—or, for that matter, in any of the myriad other worlds, planets, and moons—smells better than a good cup of hot chocolate! Or tastes better. Hold on for a moment, will you, as I take another sip. . . . As I was saying: Nothing! Not even those sanctified turds no bigger than coriander seeds which falling from the sky into the wilderness fed the famished Jews. A pretty story . . . And here's another (although I warn you, it's not near as nice):

Yesterday, as the clouds rolled into the city from the west, obscuring the sky, and just before it began to rain, I saw a young fellow, fuckable beyond one's wildest dreams, kneel before the guillotine. Now, I know that all I imagine in my worst rages is only a mirror of the world. All day, over and over again, although the rain fell in torrents and the wind sent *a bloody water surging into the crowd, Hell materialized beneath my window. At times it seemed a staged tableau, a diabolic theater as redundant as the bloodthirsty entertainments I have, poisoned by ennui, catalogued time and time again. To tell the truth, all day I wondered if thoughts are somehow contagious, if my own rage has not infected the world. I thought: Because I dared to dream unfettered dreams, I have brought a plague upon the city.*

*This idea persisted; I could not let it be but worried it like a dog worries the corpse of a cat. Such redundancy is exemplary: A machine has been invented that lops off a head in a trice, and suddenly the world is not what it was. And I who have dreamed of fucking machines, of flogging machines—I am outdone! The plague I have unleashed is not only highly contagious, it is mutable: See how it gathers strength and cunning!*

*And now—a death machine, là! Là! Just beneath my window! Have I engendered it? It seems that I have. Even the clouds pissing rain, the air filled with mortal shrieks, with sobs, the laughter of sows, seems to pour out of me. I imagine that every orifice of my body oozes crime. A lover of empiricism (and this is a tendency that, on occasion, plunges me into a fit—for I would count the whiskers on the face of a rat and weigh the dust motes of air if I thought it would lead me somewhere . . .), it occurs to me that I might find a way to measure or track this seminal poison and direct it. For the gore that accumulates like the dead apples of autumn beneath my* window sickens me, yes! It is one thing to dream of massacres; it is another to witness one.

Is this violence the bastard child of one man's rage? If so, all is irreparable, for I have imagined so much. Worse: I have put it to paper!

I recall the story of a notorious slut, Madame Poulaillon, who attempted to destroy the husband she despised by soaking all his shirts in arsenic. Arsenic she had in plenty, as rats plagued her home. (But what marriage is not haunted by the midnight chatterings and scrabblings of vermin?) It is a venerable tradition: the poison garment. There is another story of a pagan queen, a Hindoo, a real piece, who, made to marry the one who had taken her kingdom by force, offered him a robe so deadly it caused his flesh to fall away.

My mind is like these: Its poison is invisible but deadly. Far from the world, locked in ignoble towers, fed slop, forced to scribble away my precious days and years with a quill no bigger than a frog's prick—my venom soaks the city like a fog. What would things be like, I wonder, if I really put my mind to it? Could they be worse?

Ah! But another taste of chocolate, and all this dissolves. And I recall a fan you once made for the actress known as La Soubise: a fan of peacock feathers, a fan made of eyes! When she used it, it seemed that an exotic moth, a moth from the Americas, had settled on her hand. You called the fan Andrealphus in honor of the demon who was said to transform men into birds. And thanks to your instruction in the *languages of fans, when La Soubise glanced my way and, taking her fan with her right hand and, holding it before her face, left the room, I knew she might as well have spoken the words:* Follow me. *Crowing like a cock, I flew after her at once and spent a happy hour in her barnyard. (Now, there was a courageous soul who was not afraid of my reputation!)*

*Remember when I asked for a* flabellum? *How later, together, we laughed at the joke? A fan that represents chastity! That protects the host from Satan in the form of flies! Just* what *is supposed to happen, I would like to know, to a believer who swallows a contaminated wafer?*

— Have you ever been fucked by Sade?

— Never.

—You have painted scenes of unnatural acts punishable by death.

— I have painted such scenes. And I have also painted the body in dissolution. This does not make me a murderess! For exactitude, I have visited the medical school and the morgue.

— A distasteful practice for a woman! Does nothing disgust you?

— My curiosity overcomes my disgust, citizen. This has always been so. It explains, I believe, Sade's interest in me. Our lasting friendship.

— How did you come to the attention of the Marquis de Sade?

— The Comtesse Cafaggiolo sent him to the *atelier.* I had painted erotic pictures for her on an Italian cabinet, very finely made. I painted scenes of amorous dalliance on the drawers, the doors, and also the sides and top: sixty-nine scenes in all, some of them very small. The comtesse treasured it and kept it in her most intimate chamber. How citizen Sade came to see it is for you to imagine.

— Describe this chamber.

— It no longer exists, citizen; it has been sacked and burned. But I knew it well, for the painting was done there, under the supervision of the comtesse. It was papered in yellow silk and trimmed in the most tender green. Three large windows opened out onto the gardens, and the walls were decorated with copper engravings by Marcantonio Raimondi, based on the drawings of Giulio Romano. The series was unique.

— These names are not familiar to me.

— Both men were once notorious, persecuted by the Catholic Church for the very pictures once hanging in the yellow room.

From the windows of the bedchamber one could see a fountain. It was the twin of one Giulio Romano had designed for Federigo di Gonzaga. As we speak, and as heads fall beneath Sade's own window, the fountain plays even now in the Gonzaga gardens. My first real conversation with Sade took place beside it, soon after I had completed the fan. I had become the comtesse's confidante, and so it should not be surprising that we met again, as we did, beside the large *ucello* carved at the fountain's base.

— *Ucello? Ucello?*

— A winged phallus, citizen. Seeing it, Sade exclaimed: "*Fuckgod!* I like this fountain!"

— Describe your conversation with the Marquis de Sade.

— Citizen Sade called our hostess "a purple brunette," as she had very white skin with a violet hue. Unlike another woman of his acquaintance—I've mentioned her, La Soubise, whom he called "*une dorée*"—"a gold brunette," and unlike myself, who, because of my olive complexion, he called "*une verte.*" Then he shared with me some of his curious theories. For example, he spoke at great length about an invention of his: "the metaphysical eye." He likened the eye to a vortex that sinks directly to the soul, a vortex of fire that, paradoxically, is also a whirlpool in which one may drown.

He said that tears are potencies formed by the presence of light within the eye in concert with the heating action of the passions. He told me how the Maya of the Yucatán hurt little children to make them weep and so cause it to rain. The notion that pain could precipitate weather is a fascination of his because it suggests that the functions of the eye are simultaneously pertinent, acute, active, and mysterious, too.

Later, Sade described a machine of his imagination that could measure the distillation of light within the eye and the subsequent production of tears. A similar engine could measure the salinity of the bodily secretions: tears, saliva, sperm, blood, urine, sweat, and so on. According to him, the body is a machine lubricated by these fluids; salt is the fuel. He wondered about the manner in which the spoken word, producing vapor in the air, might influence the humors of others: their moods, dreams, and fantasies, the quality of their vision, sense of taste and touch, sexual desire—and also the weather.

— The weather?

— A droll idea of his: that words could produce wind. Just as the Maya thought tears—

— You have several times made mention of the New World. What has your involvement been in the production of a notorious manuscript that has recently come to the attention of the Comité?

— It is a project with which I am intimate and to which I am indispensable.

— Explain.

— Early in our friendship, Sade said I had the mind of a man. That was to say that I was fearless, fearless of ideas, which, after all, are mere abstractions until put to use. I told him that I had the mind of a woman, adequately stimulated, adequately served. You see: Under the guidance of an enlightened parent, I became an educated woman transcending the limits of my craft. My father was a scholar who, having lost the little he had, was forced to deal in rags and—as luck would have it— old books, which, after all, are often the best. So even if we ate gruel, we had books to read for the price of a little lamp oil, and that is how we spent our evenings. Father's books were green with mold; they smelled of cat piss, they smelled of smoke, they were stained with wine, ink, and rain, or spotted with the frass of insects. Many contained copper engravings and even maps of invented or vanished lands. From a very young age, I was swept up and away by a ceaseless and vertiginous curiosity. My curiosity was never thwarted and always indulged—such was my education.

— Continue.

— As much as Father loved books, he loved theater. We were too poor to ever frequent the Comédie-Française, but we saw what we could: farces performed in barns by actors more ragged than we! Or the plays took place in the back of canvas booths thick with fleas; we prepared for the evening by rubbing our feet and legs with kerosene. Some of these plays seemed wonderful to me, and perhaps they were.

Once, after a particularly mysterious performance of *Beauty and the Beast* in a barn in which the Beast's roars were made to echo horribly in the hayloft above the stage, we made our way home through streets barely visible beneath the stars and I asked my father which came first: plays or books? He thought the plays came first, the books after. And I asked him: If a thing on the great stage of the Comédie-Française was as real as he said it was, would the play have a life of its own within one's head ever after? He told me yes: just as a book lives on in the mind, mutable as the weather of one's moods. And what about the *actors*? I marveled. What happens to *their* memories? Are they swept away by the miracles they evoke? Does the painted scenery take on the colors of reality? Do the actors become all the people they have pretended to be? Father said: "Just as you, dear child, are all those beings and people you have read about in your fairy books and yet always yourself and none other, so it is with the actors."

— How did you come to the attention of the Comtesse Cafaggiolo?

— I was a gifted painter, even as a child, and so at the age of fourteen I was apprenticed to Desgrieux on the Rue de Grenelle. There I learned my craft of fan-making and was trusted with the decoration of paper and velum fans, doing drawings in ink and paintings in the Chinese manner. One day the Comtesse Cafaggiolo came into the *atelier* and fell in love with one of these. It showed a delicious little nude reclining on a divan in a garden filled with curiously convoluted trees and flowering shrubs, snakes and elephants and snails. . . . Oh! I can't recall all I'd crowded onto the mount of that fan! Shortly thereafter, she returned to take me to her yellow room, where I executed the paintings earlier described. Charmed by my capacities, she insisted I make use of her excellent library. I read avidly each night as, indeed, I always had, and became an obsessive bibliophile. So that all these years later, it should not come as a surprise that a humble fanmaker assists a notorious writer in the production of his book!

— Before we get to this book, has Sade's manner changed during his most recent incarceration?

— He is often preoccupied with the oddest concerns. For example, for several months his conversation consisted of little more than descriptive lists of ideal kitchens. He described ovens roasting day and night, ovens large enough to hold an ox: "I would have my cooks roast an ox stuffed with a pig, the pig stuffed with a turkey, the turkey with a duck, the duck with a pigeon, the pigeon with an ortolan." Along with the massive ovens, these fantasy kitchens contained great fireplaces fitted out with spits: "Sixteen spits all revolving night and day above a good, heaping mound of glowing embers, these to be attended by eight young roasting cooks, one for two spits, each naked because of the kitchen's hellish heat.

Each spit will hold three geese, sausages, sides of beef, sides of bacon. In the bakery: boys kneading dough day and night, producing buns by the hour, churning butter when otherwise not in service—"

— Sade is hungry in prison?

— Famished, citizen! He described maidens, not older than nine, shelling peas and beans, the bowls held between their thighs. White porcelain bowls, the maidens dressed in white, wearing white wimples. And scourers to scour the pans: saucepans—small, medium, and large. To be made of copper. To be scoured with sand. These scourers to wear aprons, citizen, and nothing else. "Whipped to a frenzy," Sade said, "they will scour like nobody's business."

— All this was intended to evoke your laughter?

— My friend's *intentions* have always been obscure to me. It is true he walks a fine line between comedy and terror.

— Can you tell more?

— Female cooks, big Dutch women wielding spoons—great wooden spoons as tall as brooms and good for flogging. Cupboards bursting with chinaware, silver services, pewter tankards for beer, crystal glasses for every sort of wine; a cellar brimming with barrels and bottles; the kitchen rafters groaning under the weight of hams. Dewy-cheeked goatherds too young to have beards wearing brief leathers and trooping into the kitchen by the dozens, each one carrying a young goat slung over his back. Male cooks in droves gutting the corpses of animals still bleating: lambs, wild boar, venison. In every corner, baskets gorged with onions; gravies bubbling in cauldrons; the dining table gleaming beneath spun-sugar palaces crepitating in the light of blazing candelabra; and, everywhere, freshly cut flowers. Servants running to and fro panting with exhaustion, carrying pyramids of sweetmeats on trays of gold: rare Oriental things soaking in honey, stuffed with pistachios. Marzipans in the forms of pagodas and clocks.

Every six hours, a group of fresh scrubbers arrive to clean the floor of grease and blood and cinders. For thirty minutes on their knees, these, in a lather, purify the place as the cooks, their assistants, the butchers and bakers, the goatherds and postulants, bathe in tubs supplied for this purpose and in full view of the diners, whose feasting is eternal. Sparkling clean, they return to their tasks with renewed purpose and vigor: quartering cows, skewering birds, scaling fish, glazing onions, threading cranberries, boiling jams, stirring tripe, stuffing geese, slicing pies, truffling goose liver, braising brains, tendering soufflés, jellying eggs, shucking oysters, pureeing chestnuts, larding sweetbreads, crumbling fried smelts, grinding coffee, building pyramids of little cheeses, filling puff pastry with cream, steaming artichokes, dressing asparagus, breading cutlets, making anchovy butter and frangipane and little savory croustades, gutting crabs, preparing cuckoos and thrushes in pies and cucumbers in cream, icing pineapples, lining tartlet tins with pastry dough, larding saddle of hare. . . . He also asked me to draw for him a number of gastronomic maps.

— [The interrogator looks confused.]

— The map of Corsica shows the regions for olives, chestnuts, lemons, lobster; for polenta, eels, the best roast partridge, cheese and sautéed kid; the map of Gascony shows the places where one may eat duck liver braised with grapes or a terrific soup of goose giblets.

— Is that all?

— Only the beginning! He invented a "Blasphemous Cuisine" superior, said he, to all others until contrary proof, a cuisine that is also a voluntary eccentricity born of legitimate rage.

— Explain.

— Sade invented a subterranean kitchen, a somber kitchen illumed by lanterns lit with grease, a room as black as the Devil's arsehole, a chaotic, demonic sanctuary licked by the fires of eternal ovens, ovens belching flames and smoke, a kitchen like a delirium, a blasphemous laboratory animated by nervous irritation, insatiable appetites. In other words, a kitchen in which to prepare a cuisine of righteous anger.

These are recipes of his invention: A pope, massaged by thirty sturdy choirboys for six months and rubbed down daily with salt, fed on soup made of milk, thyme, honey, and buttered toast, is roasted in the classic manner stuffed with a *hachis de cardinal* and served with the truffled liver of a Jesuit and a *soufflé d'abbesse.* The whole generously peppered and garnished with capers.

— [Shouting above an approving rumpus in the room:] All this is grotesque beyond belief!

— Recall that Sade has often been in isolation, fed on brown water and black bread. Wildly hungry and enraged, he is the victim of his own fathomless spite. Do not forget, citizen, he was fabulating, only. Such a meal was never prepared, never served, never eaten. But, citizen—it is near midnight. Does the Comité never sleep?

## TWO

Amie—

*Up here in my eyrie I consider the facts, those five days in September when Satan, disguised as a citizen, ruled Paris. And if the bodies of the victims are rotting away in their beds of lime and straw, if the courtyards are washed clean of blood and the gardens weeded of eyes and teeth, if, already, the world—always so eager to forget—is forgetting, I, Donatien de Sade, remember.*

*I remember how a vinegar-maker named Damiens cut the throat of a general before cutting out his heart, and how he put it to his lips—Ah! The exemplary Mayan gesture! How a flower girl was eviscerated and the wound made into the hearth that roasted her alive; how a child was told to bite the* lips of corpses; how one Mademoiselle de Sombreuil was given a glass of human blood to drink; how the face of the king's valet was burned with torches; how one Monsieur de Maussabre was smoked in his own chimney; how the children incarcerated in Bicêtre were so brutally raped that their corpses were not recognizable; and how the clothes of the victims taken from the corpses were carefully washed, mended, pressed, and put up for sale! The Revolution, ma mie, shall pay for itself. And I remember, hélas, I shall never forget, how my cousin Stanislas, that gentle boy, was thrown from a window the night of August tenth; how his body, broken on the street, was torn apart by the crowd. All night the bells sounded—I hear them even now. The bells of massacre. The bells of rage. "What do you expect?" Danton—all jowl and black bile—said to the Comte de Ségur. "We are dogs, dogs born in the gutter."

Already, although blood continues to spill and the trees of Paris are daily watered with tears, there are those who would say all this never happened, that the trials and executions are orderly, silent, and fair; that such stories—the head of Madame de Lamballe exhibited on a pike, of Monsieur de Montmorin impaled and carried to the National Assembly for display—are false, the fables so dear to the "popular imagination." Well, then, I ask you: If this is so, why am I, whose imagination is clearly as "popular" as the next man's, why am I still locked away?

There are days when horror has me feeling fortunate to be secreted in my tower, unseen, an all-seeing eye, remembering yet seemingly forgotten. When I leave my eyrie at last, spring will have come again, perhaps, and the cobbles of the killing yards will have been washed clean by April showers. Sometimes my tomb feels like home! For one thing, I needn't go to the window if I don't want to; I need not listen for the blade but can instead plug my ears and loudly hum; I can, like a wasp in his nest high above the world, get myself thoroughly drunk on honey. Which reminds me: I ate all the pastilles. I shall lose my teeth; no matter. Like Danton, "I don't give a fuck." What will be left to bite into? Without its kings, France will be as unsavory as America. France, too, is to be run by merchants. Merchants! I have met some—a good number—in jail. Their notion of beauty is forgery; their idea of virtue, counterfeit; their hearts are in deficit; their interests simple; their pricks as dog-eared and limp as old banknotes. Welcome to the New Century! We shall tumble into it as frightened rats tumble into a sewer. And the horrors that will be done in the name of Prosperity will make all the corrupt castles of my mind look like little more than the idle thoughts of a cloistered priest—and the excesses of Landa among the Maya of the Yucatán, a mere drop of oil in a forest on fire.

Speaking of fire: Today in my idleness I imagined a fan that could be ignited by a tear. Can such a thing be?

—Sade

— And what did you answer?

— I answered that such a thing is surely possible, like the *tunica molesta*—the shirts earlier described. I could easily imagine a fan treated with volatile poisons.

— Such as?

— Sulphur. Pitch. Naphtha and quicklime. One drop of rain and, yes, a tear could transform the fan into a torch. If the one who held the fan wore garments whitened or fixed with lime, why, in no time, he would be blazing like a pillar of fire!

— And did you make the fan?

—Yes.

— Evidence of your complicity in his murderous operations!

— [The fan-maker's brilliant laughter fills the chamber with light.] I once made Sade a fan of horn cut to resemble a turreted fortress—an amusement to lighten his confinement. The fan was *ajouré*—as are the defense walls of a castle. And I once made him a fan of ladyfingers decorated with icing; the *panaches* were made of hard candy. The combustible fan was an experiment, you see. For the book. The book about Landa in the Yucatán. I made it only to see if it was possible. Then I informed him the thing had been done: A drop of water had set it to smolder; it quickly caught fire, blazed for an instant, and was gone. And I thought that this combustible fan was like a person, like love itself. These, too, blaze briefly.

— [Bewildered, as if to himself:] How do you come up with such ideas?

— It is the nature of thought—is it not?—to come up with ideas, although Sade likes to say "I've come down with a terrible idea" the way others say "I've come down with a cold." My father, on the other hand, liked to "catch thoughts," as if the brain were a deep pool and thinking akin to fishing. But then, he was a fisherman of sorts; he fished for old books and papers, just as my mother angled for rags or, rather, the beautiful things she was able, with a gesture and a word, to reduce to rags in the owner's eyes.

— [To himself: *Mother was an illusionist.* He writes this down.]

— From her I inherited the capacity to, when necessary, forge ahead thoughtlessly; from my father, the capacity to think. When I was a girl, he had me study nature, the visible and the hidden; he had me study languages, the old and the new, so that I should appreciate the multiple paths thinking takes. I read philosophy; I have a knowledge of numbers; I am able to name not only the birds and the stars, but also the cats—

— The cats!

— Cats! Yes! Such as Tom, Tiger, Tortoiseshell, Mouser—

*Lisette!* [This shouted from the assembled crowd.]
*Grisette!*

[The names of cats cut loose from all corners:]
*Écu!*
*Choux Gras!*
*Minou!*
*Chosette!*
*Ma Jolie!*
*Holopherne!*
*Bandouille!*

— *Silence!* One might as well be among wizards and witches!
[The president of the Comité claps his hands until order is
restored.] You learned nothing from your mother?

— In our brief time together . . . [Her eyes darken, and for a
moment, the fan-maker, although standing, appears to grow
smaller.] She . . . taught me to love beautiful forms and to
recognize a free spirit when I see one. From her I inherited a
tolerance for . . . difficulty, and learned, above all, how to
inhabit time, how *not* to chew over losses.

— A thing your friend Sade would do well to master!

— But hard to master in *captivity*! Kept in a tower like a toad
in a jar! To tell the truth, Sade's capacity to think is often badly
scrambled by the inevitable violence of his moods.

"To calm the clatter in my skull," he said to me not long
ago, "to quiet my hissing nerves, to soothe my accursed piles,

I become a brainless ticking; I count the seconds passing, the minutes and the hours. To this sum," he said, "I add the ciphers my own body affords me: ten fingers, toes all pale as candles, the tongue as black as a bad potato, the nose like a bruised pear, two ears like broken umbrellas, one brain reduced to perpetual stupidity, a mood like Job's, one bunion, a pair of creaky knees, a belly swollen like a wet haystack, a cock as irritable as a caged parrot, balls like last week's porridge, teeth as untrustworthy as dice, an anus with a mind of its own. I use this number to divide my days spent in this tower, and then, by subtracting the sum of heads fallen since dawn, of letters received, dreams dreamed, of grains of salt scattered from a hard roll to my plate, of shadows leaking down the walls, I come up with the exact time to the minute of my release. Or of your next visit, beloved Comet in the Grim Sky of My Solitude. Also, the moment when Robespierre will be undone. This information I depend upon to reassure myself that I will one day feel the cobbles of the street beneath my feet, feel the rain beat against my joyous, my uplifted face, feel the caress of another human being, know the taste of another's lips, kiss the nape of a beloved neck, feel the scratch of a cat's tongue on my palm; I will awaken to the crowing of a cock and fall asleep to the sound of turtledoves cooing, cooing in the trees.

"The loss of the world has me reeling with longing. Locked away, I have come to know that the world is a food; it nourishes us. Without it, the soul starves. I feel like Gulliver caged among giants; sprawling in all directions, abundance is unattainable. You say they call me 'the Apostle of Nothingness.' But I am, if I am anything, 'the Apostle of Muchness,' 'the High Pope of Plenty and of Excess in Everything.' And if all my rights have been taken from me but one—the right to dream—I dream excessively. If they don't like it, they will have to chop off my head!

"My pen is the key to a fantastic bordello, and once the gate is opened, it ejaculates a bloody ink. The virgin paper set to shriek evokes worlds heretofore unknown: eruptive, incorruptible, suffocating."

— And brutal.

—Yes, citizen. As brutal as the world burning around us. Sade offers a mirror. I dare you to have the courage to gaze into it. [The fan-maker has totally recovered her aplomb. She is standing with her hands on her hips.]

—You dare me? [He laughs, bitterly.] Else—

— Else perish, perhaps.

— Mark my words, citizen. It is you who shall do the perishing. Now. Continue without irony, if you please. What else did Sade say?

— He said: [undaunted, raising her voice:] "And I don't give a fuck if my inventions, unlike the guillotine, are not 'useful.' " Sade is after new thoughts, you see. Thoughts no one has ever set to paper. Radical thoughts. "I am not simply dusting off the furniture!" he said. "When my pen starts thrashing, it's like fucking a whore in the den of a famished lion. The world is brimming with plaster replicas, and the point is to smash them to bits, to create an upheaval so acute it cannot be anticipated or resisted. I am after Vertigo," Sade said. "I am wanting a world in which the Forbidden Fruit is ascendant and rises just as the Old Laws fall—yes! Even the Law of Gravity."

Sade was educated by the Jesuits, who, as you must know, punish their charges—and often violently—for misdemeanors large and small, real and imaginary. One particularly crazed master, whom the students called "the Broom," forced his boys to stand in a circle and thrash one another with whatever was at hand, thus forming an infernal circle, what Sade calls "the Broom's Infernal Machine." "It seemed to me," Sade said, "that we had become—the Broom, the other boys, and I—a gear in the diabolic mechanism that makes the world spin. Night after night, the Broom sent us to our beds in pain, the lower part of our bodies covered with welts. Night after night, I tossed about in a high fever caused by rage and humiliation: a murderous rage. We had heard of a Jesuit's throat being slashed by a boy who could bear no more the blows he received. Among ourselves, we spoke of little else.

"It seemed to me that the functioning of the universe— planets in orbit about the sun, and moons about the planets— depended upon the torture inflicted upon us. I was convinced that the machine was eternal, that the torture would never end, that its end would cause the world to end. And then I wanted that desperately: wanted the world to end in a cataclysm of fire!" Already then, Sade, like Landa, longed for a holocaust.

"The night I read the transcripts you brought me of the case against Landa," Sade continued, "and reviewed the outrages he had perpetrated in the Yucatán, I had a nightmare. I dreamed that I was once again taking part in the Broom's circle of fire. As I and the other boys ran howling like beasts, weeping and foaming, we produced so much heat, so much *perpetual heat,* that suddenly the Broom's robes caught fire, the floor and walls caught fire, and then we, too, were burning! We formed a ball of flame that soared up into the sky: yellow and red, the color of pus and blood.

"Beneath us a crowd had gathered, everyone gazing up with astonishment. 'A second sun!' they cried. 'What will become of us?' An astronomer was called and arrived riding a broom. I stood among the crowd and saw that the stars on his peaked hat were peeling off. Pointing at the two suns with his wand, he shouted stridently: 'Let us now speculate upon the inevitable disaster!'

"I believe," Sade said to me, "that thanks to this dream I have seen the face of Truth. A hideous face, a monstrous face, eaten away by spite. Truth is a leper banished from the hearts of men and rotting away in exile. All that is left is corruption, a bad smell, some unnameable pieces of what was once a thing lucent and good. All that is left is a stench at the bottom of a tomb."

He told me: "I have seen a beauty's cunt worn like a fur collar, seen the bodies of wags, innocent of every crime but vanity, cut into pieces and these carried aloft like filthy flags up and down the streets of Paris. I have seen carts in the night taking bodies to graves marked only by a stench. And I ask myself again and again: Is this the virtuous violence of which we dreamed? But what else could we expect from the rabble that continues to believe in warlocks and wizards and leper kings who bathe in the blood of babes, and whispers that the nobility stuffs itself on roasted peasant boys—an extravagant piece of nonsense when you consider that the famished peasants don't have a spoonful of marrow or meat to be found on them anywhere but, perhaps, between their ears."

Sade said to me just the other day: "Everything is clear now. The plan has always been to expel me first and eat me after. In other words, like a dog, the Revolution eats its own droppings, and it is only a matter of time before I will be on my knees with my own head between its jaws. Until then I dream the same dreams as Landa, that bastard son of the Inquisition. I share that monster's fever; I am damned with the same *singularity*.

"The devastation ahead is immeasurable. I long for it night and day. Like Landa," he concluded, "I long for the disappearance of things."

⤳

# THREE

— Do you continue to work on the Rue de Grenelle?

— Several years after my apprenticeship was completed, I found a shop on the Rue du Bout-du-Monde and set up on my own. The place had seen the production of marzipan and still smelled of sugar and almonds. Better still, a swan was carved above the door. The first thing I did was to make a sign of tin in the shape of a fan. This I painted with a picture of a red swan and hung over the street. I hired a girl to build the skeletons (for by then the guild rules had changed) and hired another, a beggar and an orphan whose father had died of beriberi and whose mother of chagrin, and who, once her face was scrubbed, proved dazzling. She was quick as a whip and became a great favorite, for she knew when and to whom to show the fan with double meanings, the fan with two faces or three. She was always smiling, and this is why Sade called her La Fentine—a name she assumes to this day with good humor, as she does all else.

"It's a clean living," La Fentine says of fan-making. "You spend the day flirting without risk, you drink all the tea you want, and you never, ever need to stand about in the wind and rain. All sorts come into the *atelier,* but barbers never do, nor beggars. So I can forget that once, because of ill fortune, I lived in the gutter like a dog."

La Fentine knew how to read the eyes of the wealthy libertine in search of rarities, and the secret thoughts of the inexperienced maiden who wants a fan with which to inflame the youth she desires. My *atelier* is called The Red Swan at the World's End, and my motto, painted in a fair red color above the door, is:

> *Here Beauty and Laughter*
> *Rule all day and after*

I specialize in eccentricities, in artificial magic—such as anamorphic erotica—and imaginary landscapes: Chinese pyramids and jungle temples, a map of the world under water, hanging gardens filled with birds, and grottoes illuminated by volcanic fire. There is no other *atelier* in Paris where you may buy a fan painted with the heraldic jaguar of the New World, which appears to the initiated in narcotic dreams. Painted on green silk, he leaps across the entire leaf, from left to right.

La Fentine has turned out to be a gifted fan-maker. She and I have together produced a series of two-faced fans: The seasons are painted on the back, and the games of love are on the front. Our "Diableries" are very popular—surely you have seen these—as are our "Tables of Paris," with their recipe on one side and lovers at table on the other.

We are inspired by the Encyclopedia, but also by our memories and inclinations, those potencies that animated our childhood and the mystery of our adolescence. We believe this is why our fans are so popular, but also why we come to the attention of the lieutenant general of the police so often. Scholars collect our fans, you see, and they are often of the most vociferous sort. They engage in animated talk just outside the shop, talk the lieutenant thinks is seditious, and this only because he is too much of a numbskull to understand it. La Fentine likes to joke that the weather just outside our door is unlike that of the rest of Paris: "Hot, steamy, tropical!"

The shop is also a favorite haunt of literary madmen, some of them authentic visionaries, and others simply out of their minds. One of them, a surgeon, has been stunned by hallucinations ever since he was a child. He claims to have seen the Celestial Father, the Celestial Mother, Satan, Christ on the Cross, and a host of archangels. He came to us years ago to buy a fan large enough to hide him from the eyes of demons, to protect him from the devouring abyss of their glances, from the sulphur they farted in his face, to keep his own eyes safe from the appearances of intangible houris so captivating he feared his cock would run off with his balls, leaving him behind.

My favorite crier was the butcher's daughter Césarine, who arrived with a basket, a brazier, and a chop impaled on a fork held up for all to see. With a voice as rich as a bowl of tripe she'd sing:

> *Just like the one*
> *God stole from Adam!*
> *Buy one for yourself, sir,*
> *and one for your madame.*

—and she'd grill it for you there and then.

We also evolved our own game of Heaven and Hell. I painted the itinerary on foolscap. The first player to reach Heaven got to embrace the Virgin Mary (Sade's conceit), Torquemada, Kramer and Sprenger, or the pope of his choice. As you can see, to win was also to lose. Hell was better. You lost the game but got to screw any Jew who piqued your fancy, pantheists and Manichaeans, Ethiopians and Albigensians!

— Would you read this letter, citizen.

— I will. [She takes up the letter.]

Ma belle olive, ma verte,

*I'm so gloomy! My breeches are worn through, my stockings
in shreds, I've no ribbon for what's left of my hair, and to tell
the truth I long for something showy, a new silk coat, green
and white, with a canary-yellow lining. To don such a thing
in the morning, grab one's favorite walking stick and be off!
But I'd need clean linens, a fine shirt and all the rest, else,
even in here, and if only to myself, not to look the fool. Today,
to exorcise my demons, I itemized the things I used to wear.
How I'd fuss over my buttons! They'd have to be inspired.
My favorites were round, fronted with glass; each one contained a spanking green scarab, and all were perfect specimens.
I had a silk waistcoat made up to match with an obelisk
embroidered on each side, a sphinx at the heart. I called it
"My Enigma."*

*I had another—this one striped gold and pink with a ten-
der green lining. The buttons were Chinese—pink jade carved
to resemble naked ladies. This one I named "the China
Peach." A fellow would be beheaded in a trice if he walked
about dressed like that now.*

*These days,* ma verte, *I have the imagination of a peasant.
If a hag tumbled out of her haystack and onto my chamber pot
offering me three wishes, I fear I would be as foolish as the
beggar who wished for sausage. You know what happens next:*

*The fool's wife, a shrew and a scold, cries: "You pope's pink arsehole! You knight of the Order of Cretins! What a turd in a piss pot you are, asking for sausage when we could have feasted on roast pig! Or even the king's own* fesses *smoked like hams! I've not had a square meal since I married you, and now, when you get the chance, all you come up with is a stool the consistency of a newborn's ca-ca to share between the two of us! What a miserable goat's anal fissure you are!"*

*As you can imagine, this enrages the poor bonehead. It enrages him so much that he picks the thing up between finger and thumb and cries:*

*"I wish this sausage were stuck up this slut's nose!" And at once it is. She, of course, is even angrier than she was—if such a thing can be imagined.*

*"You miserable wretch!" she screams, the ignominious piece of tripe wagging like a puppy's tail and causing her to sneeze—and each time she sneezes, she lets go a triple salute of musketry loud enough and hot enough to cause sunspots and other meteorological disturbances. "You bishop's bastard with a stool for a brain! I will hound you till you shit pea soup and ham hocks, you dead camel!" And on and on until he cries:*

*"I wish this shrew were as she was before!" And so she is, and so they are—the two of them as miserable as they were.*

*Ah! I, too, have used up all my wishes foolishly! My youth, my passion, my promise. Today, nothing much remains but fever that prodded by unrequited appetite summons a satanic sauerkraut renewing itself as it is eaten, not one sausage crowning the cabbage heap, but forty-four:*

*Frankfurterwürste,*
*saveloys,*
*crépinettes,*
*sheep's gut würstchen,*
*pig's brain sausage,*
*madrilènes,*
*Polish sausage,*
*Strasbourg sausage,*
*chorizo,*
*boudin blanc,*
*boudin noir,*
*bite d'évêque,*
*boudin fumé,*
*marrow sausage,*
*truffled goose liver sausage in the manner of*
    *Mademoiselle de Saint-Phallier,*
*Rindfleischkochwürste,*
*sausage made from calf's mesentery,*
*dry Lyon sausage,*
*saucisson parisien,*
*Genoa salami—*

*and so on and so forth. But these are mere garnishes! For
gleaming like smiles, bedded down like houris within the
mound of glistening cabbage that rises like the tits of* la
Doulce France *in my mind's eye, are chunks of fat-studded
pork loin smoked and fresh, grilled and boiled, and slices of*

fried bacon as thick as dictionaries, and pork chops broad enough to sail the Seine on, and goose, and meatballs studded with onions, and onions as glazed as the eyes of slaughtered cows, and lastly—and thanks to Science, which has assured us that potatoes may be eaten with impunity, that rather than thin the blood they thicken it, strengthening muscle and bone, soothing the brain yet animating the intellect—a steaming heap of Dutch potatoes, yellow as butter, sausage-shaped, sweet as honey and as firm as my buttocks once were and are no more.

I'd settle for a macaroon. When I was a little boy, I was given a large macaroon stuck with angelica and gilded with gold leaf. The nuns who made it had put in all their misdirected sweetness, and I could tell that as they pounded the almonds and sugar together in the mortar they had dreamed of love. I devoured it quickly and then, because it was eaten, threw a tantrum—a rage as terrible as that initial rage of infancy when I rode poor Louis the way the Devil is said to ride the damned, my teeth at his neck, my fists pounding his ears; had I not been stopped, I might have torn out his eyes! Sometimes, I long to tear out the eyes of those who keep me here, and everyone else into the bargain! To lard my victims with their own eyes!

It is true that I have been savage, I have savaged, I have "oceloted" a number of people; it is true I was once an ocelot disguised in a dove-gray coat and carrying a perfumed fan. And that, in my fury, the fury that has hounded me all my *life, I dreamed of the extinction of the human race. But I never killed a soul, I never did to anyone more than the Broom did to me. Yet I languish here, and the Broom roams free.*

*The libertine acts upon his instincts knowing that the world is without God and that his actions are impelled by his nature. The corrupt ecclesiastic acts in the name of God to justify, as Landa did, the worst crimes. The crimes done in God's name are always the worst, crimes that the libertine only imagines in his black room lit by fairy lights.*

*Fairy lights! The words evoke the lucent years of infancy when the world was a place of constant amazement, like Lilliput. It is true I was a spoiled brat. (I was once given an entire breakfast service made of praline—cups, dishes, spoons, and forks—to coax me to table.) But even such a boy, despite swamped nerves and fits of rage (and what boy would not be frenzied by a mother who spent every waking hour on her knees sucking up to priests while his father was forever falling all over the king?)—even such a boy is eager for astonishment.*

*Nothing is known of my birth; that is to say, nothing that is known is true. Because Mother's oyster was too tightly shut to be seeded, and Father, just like the One in Heaven, no more than an Absence, I was not born in the usual way.*

*There are numerous and conflicting stories to explain the stubborn fact of my existence:*

*1. While Mother was at Mass, I tumbled from the priest's thurible and into the cleft of her bosom;*

2. I slipped out of her missal and onto her lap;

3. When on her knees looking for the scattered beads of her rosary, she heard me chirrup from under the pew.

But the true story is this one: My buttocking father, warming his balls in a brothel, took it into his head that he needed a son to fortify his line, animate his eye, stimulate his heart, and afford him pocket in his decrepitude. Thus, like Minerva, it was my fatal destiny to have been born of thought, to tumble from my father's brain into his ear and from there onto the rump of a whore. This prodigy he was able to conceal, for I was no bigger than a grain of pepper. He slipped me into his snuffbox and took me to my mother, who left her Paternosters long enough to cover my nudity with the shell of a pea and to put me to rock on the leaf of a geranium. Then she lulled me with her papist melodies, which, to tell the truth, I tolerated because I had no choice. This one fact explains why I was such a fussy baby, for if other infants are quieted with doggerel suited for the nursery, which makes them laugh and think the world a clever, funny place, my mother's attempts were so dreary I decided that once I knew how to speak I would tell her to cease her canticles else assure me a lifelong funk.

But Mother was like the Woman I Married, who, when I asked for Masters Boccaccio, Villon, and Rabelais to entertain my mind in jail, sent me psaltery claptrap as convivial as suet—the point being to keep me from thinking. (Like priests, *pious wives are made uncomfortable by the functioning of gray matter—that of others and their own.)*

*At the age of four, I decided that if God did not want me to think, I'd go to the Devil. And so it came to pass: I was made to spend my life pissing my heart out in prison! If this makes sense, then mankind should be ruled by imbeciles, which any fool will tell you* is not the case. *One of my fiercest enemies says: "Sade fills the heads of the innocent with* ideas." *I should think so! "And ideas," this bees' barber continues, "are contagious." I should hope so! But I ask you: Since the Church hates pleasure as much as it hates thought, why has God given us brains and, Heaven help us, a pair of* fesses?

*Brains and* fesses . . . *I venerate both. To my way of thinking, the one leads inevitably back to the other. They circle each other like amorous butterflies. Brains and* fesses! *These are our most precious possessions.*

*The Bible is a pile of dung. I ask you: Is it coherent? The* words *are recognizable: Nouns, adjectives, and verbs parade across the page like ants on their way to a moldering cracker. But the* ideas *are so incongruous, they might as well be written down in frass. The one thoughtful moment is Eve's. Eve, the mother of Juliette. Eve, who never asks "Why have you forsaken me?" but who walks out of Eden and climbs into bed. Eve, who, in full knowledge, fucks and engenders a world. When as a child I read about that instance in Eden when tyranny was subverted, that exemplary moment, I cried* out, "Eve was right!" and I hurled the book across the room. For this I was whipped and so it was revealed: Les fesses are endangered by the functioning brain.

My earliest memories are not of hired buffoons or of riding pig-a-back upon a poor wretch hired for that service, but of Madame de Roussillon dressed in spangles and telling stories in a hushed voice; in one, Gargantua eats a salad of pilgrims, and in another, Gulliver dances a jig for a queen the size of Cheops. Later, after I nearly ripped the prince to shreds (he refused to play horsie unless I played the horse's part), I was sent packing to my uncle's castle keep, where I often slipped away to rustle up some village brats all rough and merry. I was as enchanted as they when, in the cobbler's back room lit only by a candle, finger shadow-figures were made to dance upon the wall: Guignol and highwaymen; a witch on her way to Sabbath; La Fontaine's raven, the cheese tumbling from its beak round as a fist; Jonah swallowed by the whale. Thumbkin! Puss in Boots!

Or when Folle Blanche took us into her dark kitchen to feed us apples and omelettes and told us her "True Tales of the Infant Jesus," in which the Son of God shared the womb with kings and comets and camels, and who, while still in the cradle, shat all the way to Rome and into the pope's face.

Here's how Folle Blanche made an omelette:

She'd sauté her marrows in butter till sizzling.
With a splash of oil to keep them from scorching,

then whip her eggs till foaming.
(She'd take a sip of wine.)

She'd add some chives chopped very fine,
sorrel, perhaps a pinch of thyme.
(She'd take a sip of wine.)

Now the eggs are in the pan!
(She takes a sip of wine.)
She sets them to shiver and shake to a man!
(She takes a sip of wine.)
Then roars: "Come, boys! Let's sup! It's time!"


*She takes a sip of wine and sprinkles the eggs with salt. (The poor know nothing of pepper.) And if we eat with our fingers, we feast like kings of Spain.*

*The Romans made their omelettes with honey. If a savory omelette stuffed with lobster or ham—or both! or both!—is what I'd sell my soul for this minute if I had one, don't think I'd scorn the Roman sort, or the jam omelettes of my youth, as delicate as the thoughts of an angel, amply dusted with confectioner's sugar and disgorging strawberry jam.*

*You'd think, wouldn't you, they'd serve eggs in prison—a wholesome, inexpensive food and, if your sense is in your cranium and not in your navel, easy to prepare (although perhaps beyond the skill of prison cooks, who cannot boil noodles to save their lives). If I had a say in this, I'd assure each prison a poultry yard and, come to think of it, a trout pond, a vegetable* garden, an orchard, a milk cow. Better still, I'd supply each prisoner with his own hen. She would afford companionship, keep the cell free of vermin, and provide those precious eggs, which, as every country bumpkin knows, are at their best within the hour of being laid—especially if they are to be soft-boiled.

When the tedium of confinement proved too much to bear, the prisoner might blow out his eggs—just as the Russians do—and decorate them. The more I think about it, the more I like this idea. And a truly well behaved prisoner, although he might persist in thinking the sorts of thoughts that got him into trouble in the first place, might be rewarded for his manners at least with the gift of a goose. If he was given a potted fruit tree, the fowl could perch there. Its dung, falling as gravity dictates, would fertilize the tree, producing fruit of great quality. But for all this to be possible, a certain demand must be met: a large window, facing south, allowing the sun to enter and invigorate the living things inside the cell: bird, tree, and man.

Before I end this letter, which has afforded me the pleasure of your company for near the entire afternoon, another recollection: the little feast you and La Fentine put on at The Red Swan, the savories—aspics, crayfish, cod tongues, and barquettes—and the little cakes were all shaped like fans. You were little more than a child and I a good deal your senior, yet still a youth and unaware of mortality and disease.

I was broke. I had squandered my wife's dowry in pleasures

too many to list, and a beautiful woman sold her jewels to save my skin. I believed I lived a charmed life and knew nothing of remorse. Now, nearly thirty years later, I am old, broken, obese. But you—you are at the height of your powers, still as slender as you were, although one cannot help but notice with admiration how round your bosom has become, and how merry your eye—as if it could be merrier than it was then. How lightly you carry the years, mon amie, yes, how very lightly. I think it is because no one has ruled you, not man or god. If only you were a libertine, what a perfect specimen of a woman you would be!

You asked about my eyes. I continue to be plagued by floaters, and this because rage is a constant practice of mine, rage and harrowing fatigue. Even asleep I do not rest but continue to hear the sound a head makes when, severed from the body, it falls into its basket. My nightmares are terrible. I see an eye blooming at the center of the bleeding neck, and so affected am I by the sight I am turned to stone, a clenched fist of black marble raised eternally in anger against the world. I shall replace my family's crest with a mano in fica: that obscene hand making "the fig." Te faccio na fica! May the evil eye do you no harm!

The executions continue, and it is impossible for me to keep away. Standing at my window I am like Andrealphus; I am like a caged ocelot: I am all eyes. I thought I was a writer of fables; it turns out I am a writer of facts.

## FOUR

—You have been, often secretly, supplying Sade with books, notes taken in your own hand, sketches of eccentric subject matter including criminal acts, word lists in a language unrecognizable to the Comité—perhaps a code. All this has entered into the production of a manuscript of dubious intention. The time has come for you to describe the nature of your scheme.

— Scheme? It is only a book we are writing, citizen.

—You are being asked to give an account of it.

— Our book begins with a map-maker, a Franciscan named Melchor who had accompanied Landa to the Yucatán. Such is the map-maker's faith, and such is his vanity, that he invents all that he does not know, all that is yet unknown; invents lands undiscovered, or thickly shrouded in forests, or made impassable by defiant Maya Indians who continue to do battle with the Spanish, killing their cattle, their cats and dogs, and tearing their strange trees from the ground.

The map-maker dares not leave his rooms, but no matter: He believes his hand is guided by divine inspiration. Melchor is a madman who imagines that there where he pens in a lake, a lake must be. Or a river. Or a range of mountains. Or, if not, that these things appear once he has designated them, summoned directly from the mind of God. Melchor is a Christian, not a kabbalist, but as he studies the heresies, this Jewish idea of things appearing as God thinks them appeals to him, and he is mad enough to believe that whatever he thinks, God conceives—or, perhaps with less vanity, that whatever God conceives, Melchor then imagines. Thus the bridge between divine conception and Melchor's pen precipitates reality. Melchor is God's vessel and God's quill.

— The map-maker is mad!

— The map-maker's vanity is contained only by his folly.

He is not alone. All times are foolish, including our own, which breaks sodomites on the wheel. I ask you: Why shouldn't one mouth be as good as the other? But some times are worse than others, and Landa's was overswarming with murderously foolish men. Men who instead of delighting in new worlds drenched them in blood.

The year is 1562, and Landa—who has impressed every-one with his uncanny capacity with language, his intelligence and zealousness—has been named First Provincial. He has gone to Mani to inquire into pagan practices the Church has not managed to purge. Already a number of Maya women have had their breasts cut away and fed to dogs in order to frighten their husbands, fathers, brothers, and sons into sub-mission. Infants stuck to pikes line the road to Mani. The book opens with this image: those bodies, that road. Entering Mani, Landa sees a Spanish mastiff gnawing a human hand.

— All inventions of Sade!

— Only Melchor is our invention. But to continue: Imagine now, if you will, how such a man as this map-maker, Melchor, responds when a Maya scribe named Kukum is made to bring his books and maps before Landa; imagine Melchor's humilia-tion when Landa, to impress Kukum and, perhaps, to frighten him, unrolls Melchor's map—it is so large that it covers the entire surface of a great library table set out in the center of the Inquisitor's chamber—and Kukum snorts with disdain.

*Kukum is defiant and he is daring. He knows it is likely that he will die a horrible death. He has seen that, like everything Spanish, Melchor's map is fantastical and false. He says: "My land is not a land of dreams. It is a real place, a tangible place supporting more temples and pyramids than can be* counted, and each is as heavy as a hill. Your map-maker must take a long journey and, with his brushes and quills, put down what is truly there. But, see, he need not bother. The thing has been done. I, myself, have done it." Then, from the bundle he carries, Kukum takes out one of those beautiful books of the New World, a book made of bark paper pasted to ribs of cedar wood, with covers of cedar carefully carved—a book that opens like a fan! There, to the wonderment of Landa and Melchor, lies the entire Yucatán peninsula, the whole of the north as free of lakes, rivers, and mountains as the summit of Landa's own head. But there are tall forests clearly drawn and dry scrublands and planted fields. The sacred wells and salt pans are clearly marked, and the marshes filled with birds and fish; the cities of Ake and Chancenote, Campeche and Ichmul, Ecab, Izamal, and Chetumal are all in their places. Also marked are the ancient cities "where no one goes now," Kukum informs them: Labna, Mayapán, Uxmal, Chicheniza.

With refinement and spontaneity, Kukum had painted the features of his vanishing world. He had marked the roadways with footprints; the hills were bright with butterflies, the coastal waters filled with fish. Kukum points to these things, speaking their names with reverence: uzcay, or skate; zub, or hare; put, papaya; maxcal, yam; ixim, maize; ixlaul, laurel; nicte, plumaria. . . . Pointing to a bird painted above the towns he says: "This is the ixyalchamil, which is always there where people have planted gardens. And here is the magpie, who scolds the Spanish when they pass." Landa chooses to ignore this discourtesy, at least temporarily.

"It is painted fair," Landa acknowledges, causing the color in Melchor's face to rise. "The Indian's touch is light and vivid. But tell me," he says, turning to Kukum, "what is the significance of these signs painted at the border all around?"

"The sacred and secular calendars circumscribe the map like two snakes sleeping side by side," Kukum explains, "because the cities are all laid out according to celestial patterns and recall rituals that close and open the cycles of time."

"And these?" Where Landa points, his nail leaves a mark.

"They identify geographical accidents: This one keeps alive the memory of a pestilence—one that foretold the present time; and this carries the thoughts back to a unique celestial event. Here one is in danger of being bitten by red ants, and here by snakes."

"How often their thoughts turn to snakes," says Melchor darkly.

"Nevertheless, how clever it is," Landa responds. Taking the other things Kukum has brought, Landa has him escorted to a cell for safekeeping. "What you know is interesting and useful to me," Landa tells Kukum as he is led away. "You will not be treated badly."

"My people's memory is in your keeping now," Kukum says with dignity, as if among gentlemen.

∽

ONCE KUKUM HAS been removed, Landa asks Melchor why his map is so unlike the Maya's. "For," he says, "it is high time I told you that our soldiers have looked for the lake you have drawn so clearly and cleverly smack in the middle of the northern lowlands, and so far they have not found it."

"Each time our soldiers go into the country," Melchor replies, "they are bewitched by devils disguised as daughters of men. I have seen them return from the country reeling and laughing like drunks, and all because of the deeds of witches. For weeks they are tormented by nightmares, or sexual fire, or seized by fits of outrageous laughter, and only after their ardor is cooled with aspersions of holy water, and their minds with prayer and fasting, may they proceed with things. The lake is there; it shall be found. I, myself, have seen it and walked its circumference, which took me a full day." Melchor does not tell Landa that he had in fact seen the lake—and received it as a revelation—in a dream.

"I believe you," Landa says. "But still . . ." He fingers the map, folding and unfolding it, marveling at the cleverness of its construction. "What do you make of the apparent care with which it has been done? And this man, Kukum, is no fool, although . . . how oddly made these people are! All as ugly as dogs!"

"Ugly as their own bald dogs!" Melchor agrees.

— It is true that the natives of the New World are ugly, for I have seen a mummy on display in the gardens of the royal palace during the summer fair, and it was hideous.

— [The fan-maker ignores this and continues:]

> "Such things have been found beside their altars spattered with blood," says Landa. He lifts the map to his nose and frowns. "Just as I thought," he says. "The map stinks of copal."
>
> With growing excitement, Melchor tugs at the hair of his beard and twists and untwists it around his thumb. "A filthy thing," he says. "Its red border may be poisoned. See the devils painted all around!" Pointing to things more unknown to him and so incomprehensible, Melchor adds with conviction: "Here are the seals and characters of Lucifer and Astaroth—and lo! Beelzebuth, too!"
>
> "Faith!" Landa agrees. "I know these well, and now I perceive them! Here is the obscene character of Clawneck—so like the male genital robbed of potency by means of sorcery or, by fire, tied into knots! And here the character of Muissin—so like the buttocks of a whore! And all just as they appear in the Grimorium Verum." The lid of his left eye twitches, as it always does when he is most displeased.
>
> "See here!" Melchor whispers, because the danger of uttering the names of demons aloud is great and because his own terror has exhausted him. "See the seal of Shax—the one

*who appears in the form of a dove and who, like Kukum, speaks hoarsely. And look—the crest of Zepar, who makes females mutable so that their husbands fornicate with creatures of the deep, the meadows, the forests, and the air! And here: See those very creatures!" With a filthy finger, Melchor prods all the charming animals—the deer and turkeys and hares Kukum had lovingly scattered over his map.*

*"It is so." Landa sighs deeply. "The devices are all familiar. We have found them graven on the inner side of satanic rings and gnostical gems, or as red marks occurring spontaneously during torture beside the nipples, or upon the buttocks, or behind the knees of witches."*

*"And scratched upon the surface of magical rods," says Melchor, "and once painted on the belly of a gold-finding hen."*

*"Did the hen truly find gold?" Landa asks. "I've always thought such hens the fabulations of peasants."*

*"One in Salamanca did," Melchor assures him. "The gold it found was pure but very hot. If put into a pot of water, the water boiled. This is no* map*," Melchor says with loathing, "but only another pestilence among those—the ants, the spiders, the snakes, the winds, the rainstorms, the fevers, the necromancers and harlots—that taunt us by the hour in this unholy place!"*

*"If our soldiers are inseminating witches," Landa muses, "what will become of the world?" He is feeling peevish. Whenever one of these heathens comes before him there is*

*trouble, a stench of sulphur, sleepless nights, and the conviction that the task at hand is so vast it can never be accomplished.*

*"It is like pulling teeth from a shark," Melchor says to Landa, as if reading his mind. "The teeth grow back as many and as sharp."*

*Landa looks out the window across the courtyard, where twelve Indians are hanging by their necks. Despite the burning sun, the day is dark; the heat and light only worsen his mood. The road to Mani, as all roads through the province, has been littered with human bones; the stench of death still clings to his clothes even after rigorous washings.* It is the stench of my own death, *he thinks,* made to humble me. *Taking leave of Melchor, Landa puts on a wide-brimmed hat and steps into the street.*

*Now, it was a curious thing, a terrible thing and a humiliation, that whenever the Inquisitor walked the streets of Mani, a throng of little voiceless short-haired dogs appeared at his side as if conjured out of the air.* Why were they attracted to him?

— Is this a question for the Comité?

— No! It is a question Landa asks himself.

— [From the room:]
*Because he was a Franciscan! He stank to high Heaven!*
[The fan-maker turns. The man who has spoken stands on his chair and sings:]

Because he was a friar,
He never scrubbed his piece.
His soul was "clean"—the liar!
His soul was like his piece.

— Enough! Let us get on with the inquiry, citizens! Continue.

— [Once the room has quieted, she continues:]

*As he walks, fruit falls into the dust of the street with a wet, sexual sound.* The city of Mani is like a harlot in the first bloom of youth, *Landa thinks,* seemingly pure but harboring pestilence. *The city is like a metal mirror reflecting the blurred image of a hag who, cleverly painted, taking her distance and squinting, imagines herself fresh as a maiden. The city is like an appetizing meal, delicious and poisoned. It is a prayer to Jesus uttered by a Jew when beneath the blows of the Inquisitor's hammer he begs for his life. The city is like a lagoon reflecting stars yet harboring a venomous serpent; it is like a dream in which the dreamer is seduced and cleaves to the beautiful body that appears to be natural and delightful to all the senses but that, upon awakening, is revealed to be an illusion, the handiwork of Satan, and so the dreamer himself is revealed to be Satan's thing! Mani! Even the name causes dismay! For it is the name of that most seductive of all* heretics, the eloquent Babylonian who claimed that the Living Paraclete had spoken to him, saying that Adam's eyes were opened by the taste of the fruit Eve fed him, not closed. As if to taunt him, more fruit falls from the trees, splattering his sandaled feet with scarlet juice.

In Spain, the Devil's work was often carried out in concealment—in the dark woods at night, in attic chambers, in bell towers illumed by the stars, in barns while cattle slept, in cellars and graveyards. Here in the Yucatán, the Devil's work is in evidence: brilliant, concentrated, and amassed. The people are not like dogs at all, but well formed and comely, perfumed, their eyes like fire; the markets overspill with gleaming and curious things tempting greed and imagination. The temples, so wonderfully executed, but brimming with their idols of wood and clay, spread out over the land like a pox. Even their music unsettles his spirit, evoking lassitude and sadness, a crippling regret. Shameful to say, the little girls, dressed only in a shell and incomparably charming, cause him to falter. It seems to him that everything in the Yucatán shifts shape and meaning. Nothing is fixed. Not his own moods, nor his own understanding. The sky, too, is mutable, unlike the sky of Spain. Burning hot, the stillness of the afternoon is shattered by thunder, and the heavens, splitting apart, inundate the land with a driving rain and even hail the size of fists—spectacular storms such as those conjured by witches and described by Saint Isidore. Once, without warning, the wind lifted his *robes, and six little boys were dismayed by the amount of hair that grew in places no one was intended to see. Once he was picked up by the wind and held briefly airborne. Often the wind would carry pollen from the forests in such quantities it littered the streets for weeks on end, causing him to weep. Fruit like genitals and tongues tumbled onto the roof, making it impossible to sleep. In broad daylight, spiders crossed the road like furry hands, and large snakes were often found cooling off in the basins of holy water.*

*Sometimes, when he saw a bell rope hanging, Landa imagined himself dangling at the end. But then he recalled the nefarious influences under which the imagination—that most dangerous of human faculties—fell sway. Unchecked, it is the imagination that causes the most havoc, he would remind himself. And so he chased this image from his mind. Just as a man walking across a narrow bridge may fall into deep water and drown because of the fear the water inspires in his heart, so might he become glamorized by the idea of his own death.*

*"I must never forget that I have been sent to the New World to battle Satan and destroy the lost tribes of Israel," he scolds himself aloud. "I must be as strong as Cortés when he destroyed Tenochitlan, which was the most beautiful city in the universe."*

— Everything you have said thus far is an offense to the Truth, exotic and extravagant. Had there been cities in the New World, the Comité would know about them.

— Cortés's words were: "a city so remarkable as not to be believed." If he could not believe his eyes, citizen, why should you believe your ears?

— And you. When you learned of Sade's brutality, did you believe your ears?

— "Exaggerations," Sade assured me, the inventions of his rival, Restif de la Bretonne, "who like a dog leaves his stench and his signature—which are one and the same—all over Paris," and the lies of his mother-in-law, "a hag who likes nothing better than to chew on soiled linen." Inspector Marais was already on his tail, too; of him Sade said: "Every outlandish thing I do, I do to flabbergast Marais!"

Sade, I knew, was turbulent, but then many like him frequented the *atelier;* such "turbulence" was not unique. It is well known that the great Abbé Prévost himself indulged in the intoxications of youth, as did the sublime Villon, the exemplary Rabelais. La Fentine and I were always eager to forgive Sade his escapades when they were stylish, and to avert our gaze when they were not. It is in my nature to forgive human folly, especially when orchestrated by the passions. Even after the world collapsed beneath his feet and Sade was accused of the crimes that sent him to the Bastille, I stood by him, convinced he had been undone by calumny. Stood fast, that is, until he sent me chapters from a book, the violence of which was, to my way of thinking, inexcusable. When I wrote him a letter of complaint, he replied that he was "merely exercising his capacity to reason." I answered that the outrages he described so exhaustively could not be justified.

"The age belongs to the Encyclopedia," he countered. "It is time that outrageousness was, as is all else, examined with a cool and enlightened eye."

"You would write of pleasure," was my answer, "and instead you propose a grocer's list of cruelty. You would write of exhilaration, yet your book is as tedious as the inventory of a scullery."

Sade was furious. I did not hear from him again, nor he from me. Years passed, and I often thought of him in prison, humbled and tormented by loneliness. I recalled how in our enchanted circle of scholars, *illuminés,* exquisites, gentle madmen, *drôlesses,* wits, and mystifiers, he had always been irreproachable. I decided to pay him a visit. How diminished were his circumstances! His good humor had fled, replaced by bitterness. To make matters worse, for the duration of the visit, the one he called "the Scrutinizer" sat in a corner searching his clothes for fleas—several of which gravitated to my person.

Sade was obsessed with the injustice of his case. For near an hour he reviewed the notorious criminals of the past who had been allowed to go free. As he spoke, I was moved to pity. And I thought: A book can be a shelter. For the one in prison, a book can be all that has been lost. I wondered: But what happens when the loss is felt so intensely it turns sour, becomes stubborn rage? Then, I supposed, a book may be called a machine of war.

"My cannon," Sade agreed. "I like to force words into collision, to use them the way an executioner uses his bloody gears and blades." With energy he added: "Writing is my way of defying God. Of spitting every conceivable 'Thou shalt not' into God's face." Later, alone, I reviewed this conversation in my mind. And because I was exhausted, I fell asleep at my worktable and dreamed. When I awoke, a phrase in my dream persisted in my mind: *How can a person learn vigilance in order to seize the tiger before she herself is seized, if she does not know how the tiger hunts?*

—You have a tendency, citizen, to speak in riddles.

— Let me explain. Sade had dared take the imagination's darkest path. I thought that if I could follow that path with my own mind, I would come to understand the forces that rage about us, the terror that, even in times of peace, is always a possibility. I knew that in order to read Sade, I would have to embark on a voyage, naked and alone, without the comfort of received ideas. That in order to have a knowledge of the storm, I would have to sail into its eye. And that to do this, I would have to learn a new way of reading. And so, the next time I visited him, I asked to see the book in its entirety. In the nights that followed, I read every word. Night after night it seemed to me that I had been dragged to a nameless place in a nameless hour from which I could not help but come away profoundly changed. Sade's terrible book was like the key that opens Bluebeard's closet, affording a glimpse of the truth. Recall, citizen, that if what Bluebeard's bride sees terrifies her, it also frees and saves her.

Now many years have passed, and I have read all Sade's books, even those he himself says are unreadable. Even those he insists he has not written! They say he is evil incarnate and that his books are a plague, but I have survived the torment, the tedium, and the exhilaration of the reading that, to tell the truth, gives me the courage to live unfettered a vivid and moral life.

A book is a private thing, citizen; it belongs to the one who writes it and to the one who reads it. Like the mind itself, a book is a private space. Within that space, anything is possible. The greatest evil and the greatest good.

~

# FIVE

— Are you a Christian?

— I've had since infancy an allergy to nuns and priests. One Easter, as my father stood beside his little bookstall in the street, he was cut down for neglecting to remove his hat when a religious procession passed. I knew then that the disgust I had always felt was a gift of temperament. My favorite word since the time of Father's death is *insubordination*.

— And your mother?

— She went mad with grief and was taken to the Salpêtrière. There she perished. And now, whenever I see an execution, I say: "There's an ecclesiastical mind at work!"

— A criminal exaggeration!

—When the Inquisition pulled the teeth from the mouth of a witch in preparation for greater torture, it evoked the same Supreme Being Robespierre now embraces to justify his cowardice. Is it not a demonstration of perversity that a revolution fought in the name of Reason punishes those who rely on Common Sense? Or who imagine things differently?

— [Enraged and waving the manuscript in the air:] This is no mere exercise in imagining! It is an act of war!

—You flatter me, citizen! So it was said of the Encyclopedia! However, you forget that unlike blood, ink has no stench.

— [Hitting the manuscript with his open hand:] Some ink has a powerful stench, and here is the proof!

— [From the assembled public, a shout:]
*A stench is subject to no one but God and Justice!*
[Then:]
*Let us hear what she has written!*
[This is followed by a clamor of voices:]
*Let us hear it!*

—Well, then; take up your weapon, *madame.* [The manuscript is handed to her.]

— [The fan-maker opens it at random and begins to read:]

*Smoke rises from the square, where bodies have been burning since early morning. Some idolaters had first been condemned*

*to the stake, others had their throats torn out by dogs, and
others were hanged. One, a great lord, had been drawn and
quartered.*

— [To the Comité and, with a broad gesture encompassing
the room, the public:] I ask you if it does not already stink!

— [The citizens shout:]
*We are all laborers, after all! We're used to bad smells!
I stink, therefore I am!
Oh, what fine times, this age of smells!
Let the citizen continue!*

— [The fan-maker resumes:]

*In the dark room, a room as still as a tomb, Bishop Landa's
white paper fan shudders like a crazed and failing bird.
Landa is propped up in his bed on a number of pillows, his
shutters closed against the heat of the day—but not the reek of
hair and flesh and bone that insinuates itself into everything,
and this despite the incense consuming in each corner of the
room.*

*But for his hand that agitates the fan, Landa lies very still,
so overwhelmed with heat he can barely breathe. All around
him, devils rage, for he is hunting them down and routing
them out. Yet they are inextinguishable, as unstoppable as
fruitflies.*

*"Sancta Maria, adjuva!" Landa whispers from time to*

*time as Lilith's eighteen names, put to paper and hanging from the ceiling, float in the quiet of the evening air.*

*The truth is this: The New World shimmers and bristles with demons. One oversees the beekeepers, another the bees, another the ballplayers, another the moon. There are the demons of travelers, the demons of tricksters, of merchants and government officials. Astrologers are protected by demons, as are fools, go-betweens, and thieves. Demons oversee garden parties, funerals, weddings, and copulation. The more the bishop drums them out, the more there are: demons of Excessive Anger and Excessive Love, demons of Sour Temper, Hair Loss, and Envy. Stupidity has a demon, as do Cupidity and Revenge. The penis is ruled by a demon, as are the vagina, the anus, and the eye. Some demons wear their noses like branches of coral, some blow smoke out of their skulls, some carry their heads in their hands, and some smoke cigars.*

*The battle, which is interminable, has exhausted Landa, but the great black bed, like a bark moored in shadow, keeps him safe: Sewn to each corner of the mattress are little paper packages marked with three crosses; each contains exorcised salt, olives, frankincense and myrrh, blessed wax and bitter rue. The bed, unlike the one he had been given when he first arrived, is of solid mahogany—nothing is concealed anywhere within. The other bed, the first bed, the one that might have killed him, was laced with* maleficum. *He had spent his first night in Mani with his balls in a vise, unable to swallow or sleep. In the morning, when the First Provincial had the bed hacked to pieces, special devices the size of thumbs had tumbled out: coarse figures of terra-cotta—although he was certain some were made of human semen voided* contra naturum *and dung. One of these was the figure of a man bound and kneeling, the flesh of his face cut away, and another, larger, the size of a child's fist, showed a man overcome by a jaguar, his skull shattering within the creature's jaws. It was essential— in fact the entire project depended upon it—that the Eucharist and chrism be kept safely locked away at all times else these figurines be baptized by the witches—a thing that under torture they willingly admitted to—and, like the mares of Portugal, be impregnated by the wind. Yet, even now as he attempts to sleep, he knows that somewhere and in secrecy, women bring black hens to sooty altars. Boys—one to each corner—squat beneath, croaking like frogs. This croaking recalls the names of their gods, the demons Chak, Ek Chuah, Ix Chel, Itzamná. Above all, Itzamná—Lizard House—he who invented writing. He is their favorite, and when Landa has their hellish books stacked together with kindling and set on fire, the pagans shriek as though their bodies are being torn with hot pincers.*

*Sometimes, under the impulse of air, a book will open like a fan, and for an instant the fire is animated by imps; they swarm in the pyre as ants swarm over a corpse. Black and red, their books are so beautiful that did he not know better he would wish to keep them, to hoard them like jewels—so brightly do they shine. In truth he is awed by their splendor, their "glamour."*

*Landa knows he is causing the collapse of a world. He is burning the past, present, and future time. The people of the Yucatán will no longer know the names of their ancestors, or how to make wine out of honey and the bark of trees, to read the potencies of flowers and smoke, to pave roads and find water, to locate the places where medicinal plants grow, to tell an auspicious from an evil hour, to cure a body in pain. It is here, in Mani, that the New World will be purged of its demons. Mani means "the end," and truly God has decided it is to be the place of endings. For verily Yahweh is the God of Endings, and Death is a Power. Is it not so?*

— Is this a question for the Comité?

— No, citizen. It is Landa who is thinking.

— So I thought.

— [She continues:]

*Exhausted, Landa lets the fan fall from his hand. His excesses, the excesses of his convictions, have exhausted him. He should be feeling lighter, purer, exhilarated by the fires burning in his name. Instead he lies stricken by gravity, with-*

out radiance, flesh-bound, impure. What must he do to be pure? It is as if he must in some obscure fashion pay a penalty to his God—for the exemplary care with which he fulfills his task.

Is not the air rank with smoke? Do not bodies black with flies direct the pilgrim from Izamal to Mani? Are not the monasteries reverberating with the sounds of thrashings? And is not the mark of Cain seen everywhere on the faces of the damned? For disease burns through their numbers like a forest on fire, causing fevers and lacerations, torments unimaginable. Fetuses fall from the womb before term; at the breast, infants wither away; men and maidens in the flower of youth collapse at the threshold of their houses, never to rise again.

Is this not all as God wishes? Is it not acute enough? Has he still not pushed the limits of the possible? And if the entire world could be set on fire, would that cleanse it of sin? As Landa succumbs to sleep, he prays that before he dissolves into death, he will manage to push the world further toward completion, push it into a new orbit, one that will carry it closer to God.

He dreams:

Of things that day seen, having expected something sensibly different. A black water, perhaps; balls of hair stuck with pins; a wheel of eels. Or an explosion in the air, a sound like thunder or laughter in the room, but no. The only sound was that of the surgeon's knife cutting into the body of the map-maker, Kukum. A fluid sound, soft and intimate, a sound like that of the sea lapping the shore. One by one the organs were removed from the body and placed on the surgeon's low table for Landa's inspection. The First Provincial knows that the Devil cannot accomplish what Nature cannot, and yet he was bewildered and dissatisfied, for demons are said to leave the mouth of the dying witch in the form of wasps or flames. Recently, in Salamanca, a witch had vomited thimbles and feathers; her stomach contained an iron knife. In Madrid, another witch—a child of twelve—expelled more than twelve thousand moths.

"One could not hope for a better specimen of man," the surgeon had said of Kukum. Indeed, each object was perfect in conformation; the surgeon found no abnormalities. Landa had taken up the brain, so like a thing one might find clinging to a fisherman's net, the heart like a piece of ripe fruit, the viscera somehow familiar. The map-maker's eyelids were perfect; with the skill of a pearl diver, the surgeon removed a lachrymal sac and placed it on Landa's open palm.

"I could not be on more intimate terms with him," Landa muttered, "had I been his maker." Despite himself, Landa was moved. The Maya were men after all, not hollow bladders bloated by smoke. Yet as the surgeon continued to prod the body with his knife, Landa hoped some flame might be seen, or a black pearl.

"The body is like a maze," the surgeon said, and he gave Landa the small bones of the ear.

*"A maze without a minotaur," said Landa. "I expected you to find a minotaur."*

*The surgeon laughed. "Not a flame, nor a frog; not even a cold wind. And that is a curious thing."*

*LANDA DREAMS THAT his bed comprises the entire world. He is surprised that God had made the world so small and flat. In his dream he hears the Lords of the Underworld clamoring for attention just under him. The surface of the world is very brittle and thin, and he—fully dressed in a miter and jeweled ring, a tunicle and purple gloves, and rich vestments laden with gold lace and gems—is very, very heavy. Immobile and fearful, he hears the pope's voice worming into his ear: "Venerable brother! Heed the demons!" Indeed, the clamor beneath him has reached a fever pitch, and now he understands what they are shouting:*

His days will be dreadful. His clothes will be made of paper. There will be disputes! His lips will quiver. His bowl of chocolate will fall to the floor and shatter. His nights will be worse. He will be pursued by the night. His house will be a place of devastation where animals and men will be compelled to void their bowels.

*In his dream, Landa feels a crack, a fissure opening in the world beneath him.*

SIX

## A FISH

*The night before Kukum was put to death, he had dreamed of a tree so verdant, so deeply rooted in the ground, that it repulsed Death. Death, like the shadow of night, circled the tree but was unable to get close. The tree was so broad that Kukum, sitting beneath it, believed he was not about to perish.*

*The Indians said of Kukum: "His speech is like the Tree of Life. It is Precious Jade." Because his sermons never ended, they called Landa "He who eats his own offal twice." When Kukum took leave of his wife for the last time, she said: "Beloved, you walk too close to the fire."*

*Kukum's final words to Landa were: "I would rather hit*

*my head against a stone than attempt to reason with you."
Landa pointed to the wall of Kukum's cell and said: "Here is
an entire wall of stone. I offer it to you in parting." Knowing
he would be tortured, Kukum, already weak with hunger and
loss of blood, and fearing he might divulge the secrets in his
keeping, walked to the wall and hit his own temple so violently he cracked the bone.*

*Landa looked down on the scribe's body with bitter-
ness. "Another who has cheated the Church out of a confes-
sion," he said. "Another sinner for Hell." Then he called the
surgeon.*

*THE FOLLOWING DAY was one of marvels. First of all,
Landa had been suffering from an intermittent fever. At midnight, he thought to inscribe the secret name of God on twelve
holy wafers. Each hour thereafter, he took one of these on his
tongue, saying:*

*Hour One:*   *"When the sun burns with brilliance, I do not
              gaze upon it with admiration."*

*Hour Two:*   *"Nor do I admire the moon, even at its most
              majestic."*

*Hour Three:* *"My heart has never, not even secretly, glorified
              the sea."*

*Hour Four:*  *"Nor the sunset."*

*Hour Five:*  *"I have never once adored the stars as the
              pagans do."*

*Hour Six:*     *"Nor sensually looked upon my own member."*

*Hour Seven:*  *"Nor upon the naked body of another, unless*
               *that body was a corpse."*

*Hour Eight:*  *"I have never delighted in flavors."*

*Hour Nine:*  *"Nor perfumes."*

*Hour Ten:*    *"Nor the faces of women, clean or unclean."*

*Hour Eleven:* *"I have forever banished all licentious thoughts*
               *from my mind."*

*Hour Twelve:* *"My love for the Cross has not once wavered."*


*These last words were spoken just before the bells sounded.
His fever broke, not to return.*

*After Mass, Landa wrote upon the air, evoking the Divine
Unity with one finger, the Trinity with three, and the Five
Wounds of Christ with his entire hand, so that the air would
be received within his lungs as the Holy Book is received by
the eyes. Then, just as he returned to his rooms, Melchor,
whom he had not seen all morning, appeared like Merlin with
a miraculous tuna clearly marked with what Melchor supposed were kabbalistic characters.*

*Landa had the fish—which was so large that Melchor had
hired two Indians to carry it all the way from the market to
the friary—laid out on a large piece of clean white linen,
exorcised, and blessed. Then he stood in silence for what
seemed an infinite time, looking at those fantastic letters—letters of light, of shadow, of fire—which danced over the fish's
flanks. An hour passed. The heat in the room was intense, and*

the corpse began to smell. More time passed. The sun in its turning dipped past the roof and flooded the room with light. Melchor's feet, always sensitive, pained him horribly. Still, Landa could not tear his eyes from those letters. So intently did the Inquisitor stare at the fish that it dissolved. For a moment he looked into a deep pool of nacreous water. The day grew hotter. Melchor, feeling dizzy, as quietly as he could, fetched himself a stool, as with a whisper, a large black bird dropped down from the sky and perched at the window.

The fish appeared to swell a little. However, there was progress. As the stench, more and more palpable, informed every particle of air, the letters, elusive yet seemingly infused with life, stuttered across the bright scales with greater precision until Landa was able to read:

"Tophet!"

"Tophet?" Melchor was as perplexed as he was astonished. "Tophet?" Had he heard the word before? He thought not.

"Such as Isaiah's Tophet: broad and deep. A pyre, Melchor. A fiery trench. This is what the fish, and our Lord, say we must prepare."

"But not to roast the fish!" Melchor cried in dismay. He did not wish to eat the fish, rotting as it was before his eyes. A number of birds, all black, had settled on the window ledge to gaze attentively at the corpse.

"To roast heretics, what else? To roast pagans, stubborn as mules, mocking mysteries, worshiping stones, fornicating in the

*manner of hares, Visigoths, and Turks. For buggering their
wives, as Mahomet did; for having no laws against bestiality;
for going at it like Templars."*

*"Templars?"*

*"In other words, for coupling in the manner of Cathars."*

*"Like snakes!"*

*"Until now I melted them down in humble fires in twos
and threes and fours. But an exemplary Tophet is in store:
This is what the fish means." A flock of birds, black as ink,
as irrefutable as friars, carpeted the window ledge and the
balcony.*

*"Torment!" Melchor exclaimed, suddenly excited. "I
believe the fish says 'Torment.' " Indeed, the letters, spilling
this way and that, had shifted; shuddering like beaten metal,
the body was strangely animate. "I fear," Melchor whispered in
awe, "that having spoken so eloquently, the fish is about to
explode."*

*Landa made the sign of the cross with all five fingers before
swaddling it well in its cloth.*

*"Or is it my own heart," Melchor whispered, just loud
enough for Landa to hear, "that is wanting to explode?"*

*"A thing said to happen to hearts bewitched . . ." Landa
gazed at Melchor thoughtfully.*

*And Melchor, letting out a cry and falling to his knees—
knees already bruised and bloody from praying—took up the
hem of Landa's gown, weeping: "I must confess!"*

*Hearing this, Landa scowled. Then, with exaggerated delicacy, he rested his fingertips on the top of Melchor's shaved and greasy head.*

*Barely audible, Melchor continued: "There is a woman . . . one of their small females . . . to tell the truth, not much bigger than a dwarf. But lovely. She has come each day this week to the gate with a gift of flowers. Yesterday, I approached to see if she is as bewitching from near as from far, and to see if she is real, not one of their sorcerous illusions. Never have I smelled anything as sweet as the flowers she carried—"*

*"Tixzula," Landa spat. "A seductive fragrance."*

*"Small as she is, she is wondrously comely—"*

*"Smoke!" Landa pulled away from Melchor's grasp. "Smoke vomited from the mouth of a snake!"*

*"She is a dream, then!"*

*"The whore is Kukum's wife—or, rather, his widow. She thinks her husband is alive. She hopes the fragrance of the tixzula will soften my heart."*

*"She is marvelous fair," Melchor wept. "I am mad with longing. This I say with shame!"*

*"Fool! Do you fancy I am ignorant of your desires?"*

*"Do not think I have not scourged myself," Melchor cried, his knees oozing blood. "For the past week I have eaten green fruit and drunk brackish water! I do not sleep but each night work on a vast illuminated map of the Holy Land for the*

*instruction of the many orphans in our care. And I am paint-ing the procession to Calvary around the border as you asked—"*

*"Good."*

*"—as well as the comprehensive map of the Yucatán, which, as we speak, becomes ever closer to the truth. Yet, although I exhaust myself and feel I am about to collapse beneath the weight of my humiliation, I—"*

*"You cannot keep yourself from following her."*

*"And fearing for her! When I see how our armed consta-bles threaten her with their swords and sticks when she approaches the gate."*

*"All week she has come," Landa agreed. "She has offered me the best she has: a fat fowl, black honey in the comb, large brown eggs, chocolate, and—these past three days—flowers. These things, with my permission, the constables share among themselves. A scribe has written a letter for her, and this is placed in the basket, along with her gifts for me. A friar brings me the letter; I toss it on the grate; I will have nothing to do with her, and yet she persists. But tonight, at sundown, Kukum's body will be doused with wax and set on fire, along with the few books he, in his vanity, shared with me in order to teach me of his people's so-called 'excellence.' Yes, you look surprised, but 'excellence' is the word he used. I cannot tell you how dismayed I was by his presumption. And tonight she will be told the truth.*

"But now," Landa continued, "let me tell you a story so that you will appreciate the danger you are in. Come—" Landa designated the stool upon which Melchor, whimpering with pain, eased his bony ass. "Rest, poor fellow! What a state you are in!" Then Landa told Melchor the following story. . . .

∽

# SEVEN

## TAMALES

*"Once, Satan devised a scheme to subvert God's authority over his angels. Disguised as a soul released from Purgatory, the Enemy of Man stood before the gates of Heaven until persistence got him across the threshold and inside."*

*"The thing is impossible!" Melchor was aghast. "Why would God allow it?"*

*"The Cosmos is so vast"*—*Landa sighed deeply as if in pain*—*"and there is so much for Him to see! He cannot attend to everything Himself. Besides, if He cannot trust his own Gatekeeper, whom* can *He trust?"*

*"I thought He was everywhere!" Melchor insisted, more and more out of sorts as the fish continued to manufacture atmosphere. "I thought He trusted no one!"*

"He is!" Landa agreed. "He doesn't! But that does not mean He's got a finger in every pie and a thumb on every plum! Rest assured, however: That Gatekeeper was disposed of."

"I'm famished," Melchor moaned. "For I have taken only eggs in drink since dawn and twelve seeds of spurge."

Landa gave him a biscuit from a gilded vase to suck and resumed his tale: "Satan moved among the angels, stirring them up and driving them to distraction. He had taken the form of a beautiful youth and in seductive tones described the pleasures of the material world: silk vests, foaming cups of chocolate, and, above all, the buttocks of pretty women.

"Zélamir, always the most curious, said: 'What is Woman? And what is this Nature which you say has endowed her with Perfection? And how can this be? For God has taught us that Perfection is to be had in Paradise alone.'

" 'If you call Perfection an endless expanse of time unrolling like a clean bandage to infinity, then indeed Paradise is perfect, and from me you have nothing to learn. But if your existence is like a thin soup without salt, meat, or marrow; if, in the middle of a dark and silent millennium, you awake taunted by the thought of a palpable husk; if a static pallet of cold vapor seems a poor substitute for an animated existence upon the world's stage (so endearingly finite!), then a corporeal body and a woman are what you need. In all the Universe, she is the one object to excite cravings as delicious as is their satisfaction.'

" 'We have,' said Cupidon, 'encountered Ecstasy.'

" 'Well, then, imagine Ecstasy Manifest. An Empirical Fact. Imagine you have a Sensible Body and a prick as thick as my arm. Imagine a woman sprawled on a velvet counterpane, as eager to be fucked as you are to fuck her!'

"Relishing the prospect, the angels beamed.

"Now, with cunning, Satan had made a small tear in the walls of Heaven, which—as everyone knows—are not built with mortar and stone, but are more like a silvery membrane—"

"—Similar to the goo that allows the eggs of frogs to float on the surface of a pond, or so I've been told," said Melchor.

"Very like that," Landa agreed. He continued: "One by one the angels slipped from Heaven to follow Satan, who was already sailing toward that dark corner of the Universe where the edge of the world rises up from the muck and slime of First Causes. In a trice they were skimming the skies over Venice and then, with a great flapping of wings, came to settle at the naked feet of a courtesan, who, like the stars, had an irresistible influence over the bodies of men. Her ass, her breasts, her elbows and knees, were perfect spheres, her cheeks were like apples, her—"

"And her cunt?" whispered Melchor. "Surely she must have had a terrific cunt!"

"Her cunt was burning to the touch and well oiled, because she was a whore."

Melchor tugged at his chin with such zeal that he pulled out a handful of hair.

"Satan introduced himself and all the angels—Céladon, Cupidon, Zéphyr, Zélamir, Antinoüs, and so on—who lost no time but embraced Hyacinthe—for that was her name—wanting to enjoy her before she vanished like a dream, before they themselves would go up in smoke. For such is the nature of corporeality: here today and gone tomorrow."

"And God?"

"God looked about and saw He was alone. There was no Zéphyr to rub His feet, no Céladon to comb the curls of His beard. In a moment, he saw the rent in His walls, he saw Hyacinthe and all His angels; He saw what was what. Rising from His throne in all His terrible majesty, He condemned His angels to perpetual banishment. And because He had lost them to a woman, He proclaimed that no woman would ever enter the Kingdom of Heaven, not ever—even though Time is infinite and Eternity without end. Mark my words, Melchor," Landa continued, "Woman is Satan's most lethal instrument. The one who has bewitched you is no better than the rest, and surely worse. She is a pagan, after all, who worships the corn of the field on her hands and knees, just as the brute animals worship grass." To complete his argument, Landa intoned an Inventory of the Feminine Faults, starting *with* Avidum Animal, *passing through* Vanitas vanitatum, *and ending with* Zelus zelotypus.

*"To look on a woman with desire is to be polluted through the eyes."* Landa kissed Melchor on the top of his head before sending him on his way. *"For did not Saint Matthew say, 'Formed of a bent rib, she is by Nature bent'?"*

*Melchor tarried at the door. Although he had listened to the story attentively, and although it had impressed him, he thought that perhaps, as the Indians were creatures neither of God nor of Satan exactly but special cases, perhaps governed by laws of which he and Landa had no clear knowledge, Kukum's widow might well be as she appeared: the embodiment of modesty.*

*Seeing how Melchor lingered and the look of confusion he wore, Landa spoke again: "What does Woman do when she awakens, Melchor? Have you a notion?"*

*Sadly, Melchor shook his head.*

*"How could you, poor sod! A celibate in spent weeds all your miserable life. Here is what you need to know to kill the snake that gnaws at your testicles:*

*"Woman, having passed the night dreaming of fancies and fornications, racks her throat, snorts and spits, pisses like a sow, and, still reeking of sleep, plumps herself down before her mirror, arming herself with tweezers, hair dye, the fat of bears, paring knives, the wax of bees, cobwebs, the milk of asses, brushes, combs, and sponges. She attaches her teeth with hooks and*

*wire, dresses her hair like a salad, and glues on whatever won't stay stuck or was never there."*

"But . . ." Melchor whined, "Kukum's widow is nothing like what you describe. She is simple—"

"Nothing, Melchor, is simple! Except, perhaps, you yourself." Landa pulled Melchor back by a sleeve into the worsening air of the room and sat him down. "Why do you think this woman's skin is so smooth as to evoke a longing to bite into it as into a piece of fruit? Because she scrubs her face with a paste made of the dung of bats. And while we are on the subject, why does her hair shine so blackly? It is because of her diet of grasshoppers and their frass."

"I have seen her at market," Melchor attempted, "selling tamales. Tamales with peppers are what she eats, and she washes her face with water."

"Do you know the story of the good soldier Pámfilo, who traveled in the company of Cervantes de Salazar?"

"No," said Melchor, grumpily.

"And who fell in love with a beautiful tamale vendor? Would you like another biscuit?"

Melchor nodded and, ebbing with sleep and irritation, stuck the corroded object into his mouth.

"The tamales she sold were shaped very like the male member, and this fact, and one glance at the woman's face, were enough to corrupt this brave and innocent soldier. He bought a tamale and ate it, licking his fingers after. He bought *another; it was sweeter than the first. These tamales were so good, they melted in the soldier's mouth. The tamale vendor had a little dish of hot pepper sauce, and this she held out to him so that he could dip the tamale into the sauce at his convenience.*

" *'What meat is this?' Pámfilo asked, sighing. 'So sweet!'*

"*And she replied: 'Milk-fed deer.'*

"*Now, the tamales, the sauce, the woman's dark eyes, her smile—all were glamours, and poor Pámfilo was bewitched. He hung around the market all day eating tamales and dipping them in sauce. When evening came, he followed the woman home through the woods. Walking behind her, he could see her body move beneath the thin cotton of her dress. In her hair, she wore a* tixzula *blossom, and this, too, enchanted him. But suddenly she vanished; it was as if the forest had swallowed her whole. All that remained was the scent of* tixzula. *And then he heard a cry, a number of shrill cries, and before Pámfilo could cross himself, he was surrounded by Amazons—*"

"*Amazons!*" *Melchor was at once attentive.*

"*Amazons,* varoniles y belicosas! *Each one carried an ax of solid gold, and each one wore a little piece of moss over her secret parts. The poor soldier begged for mercy, but he was hacked to pieces anyway, his meat cooked up in a pot with peppers and, when it was tender, wrapped in masa and folded in husks. Then the tamales were stacked together in a large basket, which the beautiful Indian, dressed in white cotton, put on her head. Off she went to market to fool another soldier."*

*To make the lesson stick, and although Landa could see that Melchor was exhausted—and the heat of late afternoon, the stench of the dead fish, were dizzying—Landa forced Melchor to recall* why they were there: *not, like the addled Las Casas, to speak of love, nor, like the maniac Cabeza de Vaca, to eat ants and trade shells, but to pacify the Indians and bring them to the Light of Christ. Not much later, the things Landa said to Melchor would serve him in court, when he would be called back to Spain to face the Council on the Indies. Asked to justify his outrages in the Yucatán, Landa would say:*

• *Their gods are arbitrary and fanciful, subtle beings living in the air, filthy beings living in mud and cinder whose nourishment is the blood of sacrificed victims and the salt tears of infants.*

• *They worship vegetables and wear the heads of hares, which abound to an astonishing degree in this licentious country, as amulets; they have no laws against masturbation.*

• *They venerate the serpent of the Manichaeans and, like the Jews, circumcise their sons; they salt human meat like pork.*

• *Their lands are overrun with snakes because they do not hunt them but rather breed them in their mosques.*

• *They are addicted to their dreams, which, they insist, reveal the truth of their destinies and enable them to converse with their gods.*

• *Their perversity is insurmountable; they know nothing of logic; they are like vicious children; they despise the truth and embrace falsity; they are not susceptible to punishment or threats.*

• *Their women urinate standing.*

*"Furthermore, Melchor," Landa continued, holding Melchor up by the neck of his robe, for he was close to collapse, "the Catholic Church forbids fornication with Indians. Cortés, it is true, fucked the one they called La Malinche, who proved useful. However, she was given catechism first.*

*"And it must be added that Cortés seeded the land with statues of the Blessed Virgin—for he had the foresight to bring along hundreds of these. This in itself was enough to undo the sin. We say that this and that is so," Landa droned on and on, "that Hell contains a lake of fire, that Jesus caused Lazarus to rise from the dead, that Jonah was commanded by Yahweh to go to Nineveh but instead went to Joppa and booked himself on a ship from which he was thrust into the sea and swallowed by a great fish appointed to this purpose. Such statements are Dogma.*

*"Dogma is sustained by the true experience of Christ. The Christian, in partaking of Christ's blood and flesh,* embodies *Dogma: His experience of God is visceral.*

"Whereas the pagan relies upon figments to rule him and so is easily deceived. Figments replace facts for the Indian, and that is why they belong not in the mind, *Melchor,* but in the fire.

"Finally: If Christian Faith were not superior to pagan figment, the Indians would not dry up before the Glory of the Church like toads in the sun. For do they not die in droves? Are not their numbers dwindling as we speak? Are not their mosques in ruin?"

As if in agreement, the many birds at the window all cried out together before clattering off. Surely the stench of the fish, now unbearable, had convinced them it was no longer worth hoping for.

## EIGHT

— Citizen, the Comité wishes to inform you that this is your final day of trial, perhaps your last hour.

— My last hour? Or the last hour of my trial? [She clenches her fists, perhaps to keep from trembling.]

— Most often the two coincide, although not always. [He sighs, as beneath a great burden, and, leaning forward, speaks. His voice is thick and strange, as though his tongue is swollen.] In gardening, as with digestion, rot is a necessary and natural process. It results in a fertile rose bed, a healthy constitution. The text under scrutiny—your text—is rotten and unhealthy. There is nothing natural or good about it; it is not representative of a natural process—

— [From the public, a stamping of feet. Someone shouts:]
*Get on with it!*

— It is representative not of the human spirit's vast capacities
but, rather, of spiritual vice—

— Spiritual vice?

—Vice! Of the spirit or, as in this case, spirits—as there are
two authors responsible, not one. The language is excessive,
obscene, peculiar. . . . The representation of the Creator—

— [From the public:]
*The whore's an atheist! Get on with it!*

— The idea of the Creator has, since the Revolution, under-
gone a certain *beneficial evolution*. . . . But our understanding of
Him, intact, is treated here with what can only be called perversity, a . . . perverse impiety. The book is an example of—

— Spiritual vice. [This said with irony. Yet she is pale, exhausted, out of patience.]

— [He rises, threateningly, waving papers in the air above his
head.] Certain documents have come to our attention! More
documents! [He continues to rattle these about so that they
are visible to the crowd. The public is curious and the room
surges with a dull roar.]
    Truth is never found in Consequences! [He is shouting
above the noise in the room; this bit of nonsense is lost in the

hubbub.] One more head severed from its body will not further Truth! It is Causes, citizens, Causes alone . . . and the
Causes of the Consequences are about to be revealed *in these
documents*! [The public, perplexed and expectant, quiets down.
As he reads, the fan-maker visibly reddens, especially her ears,
which turn crimson as though they'd been boxed. As her dis-
comfort grows, so does the noise in the room, rising again like
a swell of dirty water, punctuated by insults.]

What are the attributes of the ideal woman, the true
patriot?

— [From the public:]
   *Qu'elle ferme sa gueule!*

— [He raises his hand to silence the room and reads:]

   *Citizens, as you know well, I spend my days and nights wan-
   dering the streets of my beloved Paris, peeking in here, listening there; why, I am the eyes and ears of Paris! And my Paris
   is the people's Paris; I move among those inspired and generous souls, those fearless souls who have seized the day and
   made it theirs. I am proud—you know me well—to consider
   myself one of you and your equal.*

You recognize the author, citizens, a man beyond
reproach.

— [From the public:]
   *Restif!*

— Restif de la Bretonne, yes. To continue:

*But what of the women of Paris? But what of those women
who belong not in our dreams, our hearts, but who instead
haunt our worst nightmares? What of them? This, citizens, is
what I have, in my most recent peregrinations, seen:*

*A woman who continued to make a very good living
indeed, sewing pearls to velvet slippers and gold lace to silk
sleeves—in the old manner (for yes! there are still clients for
such fripperies as these!)—and who spent her nights in the
arms of a foreign merchant. In cruder terms: A bit of pork disguised, was, just the other day, routed from her atelier by a
band of patriotes who had had enough of the creature's
haughty ways, routed from her atelier, I say, like a weasel
from its hole, and given a public thrashing to put the fear into
a bison! To my mind they were generous: The trollop deserved
more.*

— [From the public:]
*She deserved to lose her head!*

— [He resumes:]

*What is worse, all the time she continued her miserable and use-
less trade, carousing with strangers, eating chicken in delicate sauces
while the rest of Paris starves, she openly mocked the people, mocked
their callused hands and rough ways. "Let them wield their washtubs*

*and pitchforks!" said she. "I shall continue to thread my needle!"*
*Well! She will have to thread it standing up for a good time to come!*

— [Stomping in the room and much laughter.]

— [He goes on:]

*Another example: A loudmouth, a so-called woman of*
*sense and lover of liberty, was daily infecting the galleries and*
*podium of the National Assembly with her strident cries for*
*"feminine freedoms," while her husband, a combatant who*
*had lost a leg, was left alone at home in a filthy bed without a*
*kind word or a spoonful of soup. Passing by his house, I heard*
*his call for aid, and entering a squalid place that surely had*
*never been swept, I made the poor soul a tisane. (I always*
*carry a little pouch of herbs on my person for such occasions.)*
*Hearing weeping from a dark and dismal corner of the hovel,*
*I found two little ones, one in fever crying piteously for her*
*mother, and both half dead with hunger. I quieted them as best*
*I could, and cooled the elder's fever—she was no more than*
*five—with a compress of cold water I fetched from the public*
*fountain a good way down the street. (There was no water in*
*the house, nor was there anything to eat!) Then, fetching fresh*
*eggs and butter from a grocer, I fed the little family. I did not*
*leave them until I was satisfied as to their comfort, and had*
*promised to find the wayward trollop who—all the while she*
*was spouting the word "Liberty"—kept her family in misery.*

*I took myself to the Assembly—she was not there—but found her, at long last, at one of the hermaphrodite clubs that have sprung up all over Paris like lethal mushrooms.*

*"I'm looking for Madame L——," I said to the creature who opened the door, and in a moment found myself confronted with a very ugly woman in trousers, her mouth deformed by a pipe.*

*"Madame," I said with feigned civility, "I have only just left your husband and children. Your house is in ruins, your elder child is in fever, your husband is in pain—his leg is gangrenous—the baby is in tears." I saw that our monster looked at me with surprise; she was, despite her inebriation, attentive to my words.*

*"You have seen them?" she asked, astonished.*

*"Not only have I seen them," I replied, "but I have fed them, dressed your husband's leg, and soothed the child's fever." These words touched the witch's heart, and she fell to her knees, sobbing.*

*"Ah! Thank you, monsieur!" she said when she could. "But why have you been so generous? Are you a friend of my husband's?"*

*"I never saw him before in my life," I said. "But yes, I am his friend; I am friend to all men who have been left to rot by their wives—wives who have no place in the violent discussions of the Convention nor in illicit cafés! Wives who belong at home, looking after the men who defend our Nation; looking after the future citizens of France!"*

"*What you say is true!*" *she exclaimed, wetting my sleeves with her tears.* "*And wise! I will go to them at once!*" *As she hurried off, I saw her toss her pipe to the street, where it shattered.*

*Citizens, my tale has surely dismayed you, but it has warmed you, too. However, my tales do not always comfort the soul. Here is my third example:*

*A certain fan-maker—*

— [At these words, the room seems to explode. The fan-maker puts her hands to her ears and for the first time appears to lose courage entirely. She also closes her eyes.]

*A certain fan-maker, who continues to find clients who can afford taffeta and ivory, was seen with the notorious Olympe de Gouges in the botanical gardens, kissing in full view of everyone—including some very small boys who, in their dismay, thrust their little faces into their hands and sobbed, and a little girl whose virginal nurse, equally upset, picked her up to make a hasty retreat. Now, it may well be—surely it is so— that women belong to the human community, as Olympe de Gouges insists, that they are capable of reason and deserve to be included in the Declaration of Rights. It is, however, one thing to be capable of reason, another to be reasonable. Is it reasonable, I asked myself, to flaunt perversity in public?*

*Finding a large bucket of rainwater, I used this to cool the* lesbiennes' *ardor.*

*"How dare you!" they cried, leaping to their feet, as sopping wet as at the instant of their birth.*

*"How dare you, mesdames," I replied, "deprive the New Nation of citizens?"*

— [The room resounds with cheers. With effort, the fan-maker opens her eyes. When the room falls silent, she speaks.] You are toying with me. I will answer no more questions.

—You will tell us about your "friendship" with the woman who has been named, an agitator who has—

— I will not.

— Olympe de Gouges.

— I refuse.

— [Lifting the document up in the air and stabbing it with a grubby finger:] This document is several years old. It is our understanding that you have not seen Olympe de Gouges for some time. By speaking, you— [She has turned away, her eyes to the floor.] Look at me! [She closes her eyes.]

— [To the guards:] Open her eyes! [One guard holds her, the other pries her eyes open with his fingers, tearing flesh. She cries out.] There is no longer a reason to protect her. Your lover, Olympe de Gouges, was beheaded this morning.

# Part II

# LES
# DRÔLESSES

*Against the disease of writing one must take special precautions, since it is a dangerous and contagious disease.*

*—Abelard*

≈

# ONE

*3 Brumaire—the Season of Mists! 1793*

Sade, mon ami,

*There are not many ways for a woman to respond to inhumanity. One may, as Théroigne de Méricourt, be driven mad by a public spanking and finish one's days shitting and sleeping on a pallet of rotten straw. Or, like the inimitable Charlotte Corday, coiffed and dressed in Indian muslin, choose to plunge a new knife into the heart of a butcher. One may also, as so many have these past months, take one's life. Incapable of murder, refusing suicide and insanity—as tempting as they are—I shall do as you have done. I shall write a letter.*

*I believe this is to be my last night. To exorcise my anguish, I shall write to you. To exorcise my anguish and to conjure Olympe de Gouges, who—it occurs to me—is just moments away. If those moments were ahead rather than behind me, I could dream of seeing her again. And you, in your tower, tearing the world to shreds and putting it back together in radical conformations unlike any imagined before: You, too, are moments away. If I cannot dream of seeing you either, at least I can offer you this night. It is a moonless night. It is also very, very cold; my cell is not provided with a stove.*

*It is hard,* mon ami, *so hard not to tremble!*

*The lens of memory is often cloudy; it may be stained with tears or blood, grow dull with neglect; it may shatter. But these things I choose to describe to you—for it is not impossible that you shall be the one to survive all this—could not be more tangible. That first night opens out before my mind's eye like a fan of silver painted with one of those marvelous Italian landscapes that are not rough approximations of the truth, but instead evoke the softness of the air and the scent of roses. With eagerness one is made to gaze upon a fictive horizon and dream. (What I would not give to hold such a fan tonight! To paint one!)*

*But for now, just imagine:*

A PORTRAIT OF OLYMPE DE GOUGES

*(painted on a fan of silver, its* panaches *of fine ivory)*

*A black felt hat perched with provocation on her mane of black curls, a bewitching cast over one eye, her breasts balanced* beneath her collarbones like bubbles of glass—she sweeps into the atelier on a winter's afternoon. The year is 1789, and the Revolution holds such promise! In the background, La Fentine is speaking to a customer, and I am painting a border of grapes and vines.

You would like her. You would call her "une amazone," "une noire." You would admire her unique brand of heresy, her eccentricity. Olympe is vain, generous, voluptuous, and unstoppable. She is capable of dictating a play in four hours. She believes that life is tragic, liberty worth its intrinsic risks, and the Marvelous the greatest treasure of the sovereign imagination. Like you, she insists on the necessity of plea- sure. And she entertains a passion for erotic imagery; this is what brings us together. The little series you inspired, those "illicit" delights, are combusting in the hands of courtesans and mondaines in such quantities that not an afternoon passes without a girl in red skirts storming the atelier for a purchase.

"I'll take this one," says Olympe (and her voice is the voice of a child), snapping open a scene of fellatio into the startled face of a prude who leaves the shop in a huff. "The only differ- ence between a prude and a hussy," Olympe declares, the dim- ple on her cheek attracting my immediate attention, "is the same difference one remarks between the artist and the ama- teur." What a talker! For a moment she gazes into my face.

"You have a rare radiance," she declares, causing me to laugh with surprise. "I will call you Solaire."

*"Call me Solaire," I say, put off by her presumption, "and I will call you La Grande Folle."*

*"Fan-maker," she says with wounded eyes, "do not be unkind." It seems I have hurt her to the quick. "I wish for us to dine together," she whispers, pressing her card into the palm of my hand. "Tonight." The black plume on her hat trembles. "Unless you are a capitalist? I do not dine with capitalists!" Again, I burst out laughing. "No," she decides, one eyebrow raised, her smile searching, ironical, and sweet all together. "No. Clearly you are not a capitalist!" Her purchase pressed to her bosom, she whispers: "Nine." When the door rattles shut behind her, the bell all a-jangle, the room bubbles over with La Fentine's laughter.*

*"I won't go!" I decide, furiously blushing. "Anyone can see she's spoiled! Anyone can see she's used to getting her way!" But La Fentine only laughs more merrily. "Don't be such a tight ass!" she says.*

And so Gabrielle went. Somewhere I've a letter from that time. . . . It may be here still, although so much has been seized. God's Balls! It's enough to drive a man insane. Just last month these things were taken from my cell:

• *a small bronze statue of a hermaphrodite bought in Florence in my youth (my last* objet d'art*!)*
• *an incomplete manuscript describing the sexual initiation of a young Cathar into the inspired art of buggery*

- *a packet of chocolate saved against a day of deepest misery*
- *an entire year's worth of nail parings, the object of an (as it turned out not especially interesting) experiment*

(So much has been taken from me that loss is a dull, if constant, irritation—much like a toothache.) But where's that letter? As I recall, Olympe de Gouges—a "notorious loud-mouth" and a mediocre writer—was living on the Place du Théâtre-Français, the better to get her fearless and, to tell the truth, dreadful plays produced. Hair flying, wearing red pantaloons, she opened the door. Although it was winter—the terrible winter of '89—the heat inside was tropical. Designating an aviary, the first thing she said to Gabrielle— clearly rehearsed—was "The Torrid Zone is their chief seat." Yet my understanding is that if so much of her was fraudulent, Olympe de Gouges was truly . . . *insolite.* She said things worth repeating, such as "I am a Creature of Nature, as Changeable as Weather." A thing I, myself, might have said. Or this: "We admire Nature's variety and accept the flowers in their multiplicity of colors; indeed, if all flowers were white, we'd love them less. The world is richer for Nature's permutations, so why, tell me, do we not accept diversity within our own species?" It would do well to come up with an example of what I intend by "*insolite.*" Because, as Gabrielle noted, she was, at her best, an eccentric. Ah! I recall this (although I cannot remember the context; I do know, however, that it was the sort of thing that endeared her to Gabrielle):

"I often wonder: If every living creature on the face of the planet moved to the North Pole, would all that heat melt the polar ice? If so: Would Paris be submerged by water?" And this (it is extraordinary how, once the mind has embraced a task, its gears and wheels are set to spinning!—despite a rotten mood and without a cup of chocolate!):

"It is usual to think that perfect beauty is masculine since the so-called Creator is male—or so some like to think. But the scholars all agree: The origins of everything are *celestial*. And, did you know? The stars are, each and every one of them, *hermaphrodite*!"

This is an intriguing idea. More interesting in its way than the old Babylonian quackery that the stars influence life of the planet or that a stellar cataclysm will produce prodigies. (If so, at my conception there should have been a stunning meteor display. There wasn't.)

"I do not believe in God," she told Gabrielle that first night, "but in starlight, the stellar wind, the insistent energy of the Heavenly bodies as they converse in Ether. I am certain that if we could navigate Infinity, the closer we'd get to the stars, the more we would feel at home."

# TWO

One very long day on the heels of another; one very long night.

THE EYE IS active: It tigers the mind. It feeds on light, is informed by shadow. And if it is so that the eye can "kill with a glance," a horrendous sight can cause a stalwart man to fall over stone dead. Not stalwart, I stay away from my window.

*SOLVITE CORPORA ET coagulate spiritum.*

IF, AS SOME think, Nature needs to coagulate, corrupt, and dissolve in order to renew Herself, then shall I, having rotted away, be born again? Will I, after so much suffering, and with the help of a sound digestion and the philosophical fire, become *perfect*? Or simply *more corrupt*? You see: Suffering makes the spirit mean. It impoverishes the heart.

Many are the days when I become so crusty that I fear I will calcify or, perhaps worse—surely worse—turn to mud. I prefer calcification. To be a kind of aggregate of crystals; to, in other words, achieve an optical quality and, like the Maya shamans, a certain *transparency.*

To be *prismatic* in habit! To be . . . reticulated. To be studded with bright angles. My girth has imparted an unavoidable *opacity;* I am in a chronic state of eclipse. If I could, I would choose to be formed of rock crystal, to be, there and here: water-clear! Chemically pure: lucent, refractive, prismatic. Ah! To be *prismatic:* splendent, a changeling. To glimmer.

Then again, one might be graphite—a good conductor of heat, if I remember well. *Magnetic!* To be, like amber, electrified by friction! To be of malachite: *always green.* To be a malachite dildo up the ass of a youth handsome in the extreme. To be gold: a gold ring on the finger of an inexhaustible *branleur. Mais oui . . .* to be anything but mud!

I HAVE PAWED her last letter; I have worried it as a dog worries a rib; I have wept over it as though we had been lovers; and I have pondered—all night I have pondered—knowing full well how preposterous it is, a total waste of time: the reasons, the Unreasonable Reasons, for her execution. I know our friendship is in part to blame; the Revolution has

embraced sexual prudery with the same passion a necrophil-
iac embraces corpses. So there's a reason: *friendship with Sade.*
Further: I've been told our little story of the Inquisition in the
New World has offended the Powers. (The Comité is made
up of men who do not read, except the books they burn.)
Now that Robespierre has embraced that bum-cleaver
Yoweh—this rumor is more a certainty. Lastly: *her affection for
women.* Above all, her brief liaison with Olympe de Gouges,
who wrote a play to glorify D—— before he proved himself
a traitor: foolish mistake! A terrible play, I hear, yet people
write bad plays all the time. Nothing comes more easily; I,
myself, have done it. Surely she wrote the play to prove her
patriotism—now, there's a thing one should never do! What a
trap *that* is! What it means to be a patriot changes from one
instant to the next, and women have lost their heads for less.
An example: a lady of my acquaintance who was seen eating
a flan with a *député* out of favor with Robespierre for dressing too smartly and whoring. Both dispatched *sans un mot.* If
it is possible to lose your head over *chemises* and *foutre*, well,
then, surely a *play . . .* !

Worse, really, is the Other Thing: Illicit Delight.
Robespierre—I know his type well—hates a good time.
Olympe (that silly name of hers!) and Gabrielle were lovers.
Perhaps they flaunted it. Or, simply: *were seen together.* Once by
the son who—I've a letter referring to this somewhere—
came in upon them as they slept, sweet as lambs, in each
other's arms. The boy in boots, back from the wars, famished,

blundering in and roaring them awake, *roaring,* wrote Gabrielle, as though *in the throes of a Catastrophe!*

And they were seen many times by Restif, which was inevitable because *he could not keep his eyes off them!* The thought of those two lionesses devouring each other, solarized by desire, was a hot magnet that caused his rusty article to wag and to weep. Imagine him for an instant if you will: Crouching at some spy hole or other, his brain in a boil, Restif stares and stares—he cannot help himself! His loathing is a sort of worship, you see. He's crazy to encunt the two of them! Instead he's reduced to spying: now manipulating his little faucet, now his little pen, no longer in possession of his wits, scandalized by the two "notorious loudmouths" who go at it with hilarity, tenderness, and ingenuity. Ah! Ah! His fuck is flying!

Now that he's emptied his balls, the Owl of Paris is replete with scorn. Off he goes to publish another broadside against the two, posts some, hands more over to the booksellers, and then, having supped on fresh peas, finds a little whore to frig him. Damned! Tonight in my loneliness, the certitude that Restif ambles my beloved Paris—Paris! her mysterious doors! behind each door a lass with a beautiful ass, a green footman as fuckable as my beloved La Jeunesse! each door like the cover of a forbidden book to be opened! each lover within a book to be read, a book to be written! Paris!—that *he,* the ignoble Restif, splashes about freely in the filth of his own making, like an infant making merry with his waters and turds, while I am contained like a thing in a box—so wretched a box! so wretched a thing!—throws me into such a temper that I am reduced to trembling with rage and cannot write without breaking the nib of my pen!

Peeping through holes is a singularity of taste I can well understand *when it takes place in a brothel*. Once, long ago . . . Ah! There it is again: the specter of the Lost Manuscript! I itemized a hundred things, each more outrageous than the next, that one might imagine peeping at through the apothecary keyhole. I included the tale of a libertine, hated for his miserly tips and glacial ejaculations, receiving the gift of a blazing hot fart well peppered with pimento in the eye. A touch of realism: One frolics with whores at one's own risk. (No one knows that better than I! Whores and a strumpet sister-in-law as beautiful as the day— these are the items at the top of the list of my undoing!) And here, in passing, forthwith, and for the gracious reader's enlightenment, are listed the

RISKS OF BROTHELS
1. the clap
2. running into a lady of one's acquaintance, slumming
3. crabs
4. being robbed of one's watch and shoes
5. a sound but altogether impromptu and undesirable thrashing
6. the pox

7. a jealous pimp armed with a knife

8. *le chancre mou*

9. to be ruined by a sumptuous *baladeuse,* or a well-hung *andrin*

10. *above all:* to be peeped at by some masturbator who has paid more for his hour's pleasure than you have—Restif himself, perhaps—and who as he watches your ignorant bum rattles his own device!

Ah! Ah! Ah! Perish *that* horrid, horrid thought! (And here you have jail's greatest mortification: the fact that one's thoughts cannot be aired out, not ever! And so one cannot help but think such things, to stew and pickle in them. Because once they are thought up, there's no forgetting them! That is, not until an equally disagreeable idea attaches itself to the brain like a tumor.)

Olympe had enraged Restif, and how? I know the facts from Gabrielle:

He had followed her into the Jardin des Plantes. Suddenly, there he was, bowing and beaming in the path's turning, complimenting her on a pamphlet she had just published but which, it was clear, he had not properly read, and commenting on her attire:

"Carmagnoles! Carmagnoles! Everyone is wearing carmagnoles! But you, *madame,* are the only one to carry it off!"

Restif proposed a cup of coffee at the fashionable M. Pickersgill, which had just opened and was all the rage—with its murals depicting Captain Cook trading in beads in Otahiti; the beauties of the Bay of Matavai, Tropical Scenes including natives riding the waves on flat pieces of wood (a thing, I hear, still causing much animated discussion), and pictures of the Adventure and the Resolution sparkling beneath the tropical sun.

"The coffee is hot, the pastry excellent, the murals *must be seen,* the conversation—as you, dear *madame,* and I will be its principal authors—will be sublime. *Alors!* What do you say?"

"I hear you have already etched your name into one of those famous murals," Olympe replied in her driest tones. "It seems no place is secure from that maddening habit of yours. Indeed, you brand the streets and sights of Paris with the impunity of a gaucho branding cattle! I was sitting in a pretty little *cabriolet* the other day, its doors nicely painted, and there saw carved into the wood beside me your initials, the date, and the cryptic message: *The Wheel Has Turned.* 'The Wheel of megalomania,* for certain!' I said to my companion, who informed me that her favorite bridge flourishes no less than six of your portentous graffiti! You have, sir, in a silent medium, begun to create a certain cacophony that I, for one, resent."

Restif trotted off as fast as he could. Later, when Olympe left the gardens, she saw a gentleman standing before a large oak tree freshly carved with the pest's initials and the date, and

---

*Megalomania: a marvelous word, and surely of her invention.

a phrase she could not decipher.* She asked that it be read aloud; the gentleman obliged:

*"L'eau des marais n'est ni saine, ni claire, ni agréable à boire."*

"Little does the scurvy creature know how sweet it is to drink from your cup," Gabrielle would tell Olympe when she heard the tale. "But I shall fear for you, knowing how Restif hurt my friend Sade, who, at this moment, languishes in a tower, and this in great part because of Restif's fabulations. He is as much a chronic *mouchard* as he is a slanderer, and a defacer of public property."

"It is true," Olympe sighed, "that before he scrambled off, he looked at me with such rage that I am certain he would have—if he could have—had me sent to Salpêtrière at once to be chained inside a kennel."

"It has happened to women as spirited as yourself," Gabrielle replied knowingly.

Having told Gabrielle her story, Olympe de Gouges was eager to hear mine.

"It's an old story," Gabrielle told her, "most recently revived by a fiction of Sade's that reveals to the utmost degree the horrors of incest, and although as yet unpublished, a manuscript is in circulation. Everyone knows of Restif's incestuous behavior—"

"Not I!"

---

*Although a famous wit, de Gouges was unschooled and could barely read and write when this incident took place. *She dictated everything!*

"One night, Restif awoke his eldest daughter lustily with kisses. In his excitement, he forgot the candle he held in his hand and set fire to his wig! His wife came running, and the Owl of Paris spent the night in the street in his singed wig and *chemise.*"

"Well done!"

"Restif—whose nose, like a street dog's, is everywhere at once, and whose entire *oeuvre* is an act of self-justification—"

"When it is not *glorification!*"

"—is convinced that Sade is pointing his finger—"

"The manuscript's title?"

"*Eugénie de Franval.* Restif blames Sade, as do so many others—and I cannot stress this enough: as do so many others enfevered by Restif's lies—for what he calls Sade's 'aberrant and violently disordered imagination.' "

"And Sade?"

"Sade says: 'My imagination is aberrant, *perhaps:* but it is *mine.*' " (Exactly so!) " 'A man—especially one denied access to the world and its diversity, its infinite pleasures and even its pain' "—(for yes! here in my tower, steeped in despair and humiliation, the pain of Real Life evokes wistful longing)— " 'a man, I say, has the intrinsic right *to imagine!* If they wanted to keep me from dreaming nightmares, they should not have locked me up! The less one acts, the more one imagines, and that is the truth. And so, here I am, instead of wenching, writing books fit to plague Mephistopheles Himself and all his troop of lesser demons!' " (How well she quotes me! How carefully has she read my letters! Ah! My exemplary fan-maker!)

"And you, lovely Gabrielle," Olympe says, pressing—or so I imagine—her lips to Gabrielle's wrist: "What do you think of this fiction that so maddens Restif?"

"Sade worships ambiguity. In other words, the story never settles down, but teases the mind incessantly. The end is weak"—(she's right!)—"but I suppose he bent to the demands of propriety"—(a hateful thing for a writer as inventive as I am and as angry!)—"in order to publish the thing."

"Already I like him less!" (For this, Olympe, I like you more!)

"Yes. Well, but listen. Within the tame frame of the tale's beginning and end, the writing is outrageous and stunning."

"Fit to plague Satan?"

"Fit to plague Satan, my dear Olympe. And this, in part, because it is so, so . . . ambiguous."

"You have me curious. Go on!"

"Eugénie's father, Franval, educates his daughter admirably, *completely,* thus demonstrating that when given the chance, women are as intelligent as men, as capable of aesthetic, philosophical, and scientific inquiry."

"I wish my father had thought as much. You see: I am for all practical purposes illiterate. Everything I know I have overheard, or it has been read to me. I am from the Midi; my

French is, I know it, horticultural! One critic calls it 'menstrual'! I know nothing of style beyond the embellishments the grandmothers of Toulouse use to color their fairy tales, and village boys their lies. I am the bastard of a nobleman who abandoned me because I was born female; I believe a bastard son would have fared better. Whatever the truth of that, his abandonment assured I would grow unschooled. When I found myself alone in the world with a child of my own, I requested my father's aid so that I could educate myself and overcome the obstacles imposed by illiteracy."

"And his response?"

"'Cosmic order,'" Olympe lisps, her hands raised foppishly, little fingers curled, "'depends upon the void that fills the heads of pretty women.' I told him that only knowledge can assure the world's happiness. Ignorance, I am convinced of it, engenders Monstrosity."

"A good answer!"

"Yes. I was *spirited* even then. And, since a first brief marriage forced upon me, I have lived unfettered by the laws of husband, father, or priest. *Spirit* is my strength, but if I dictate my pamphlets and plays with passion, still they swarm with errors. I cannot check on the orthography of those I pay to take dictation (and I cannot pay very much!). My enemies seize upon such errors as the proof of my poor judgment. Ah! But we are forgetting Eugénie, and I am eager to know what happens to her."

"The girl's education is in no way hindered by the gibberish of priests. She is a perfect little atheist, a freethinker and a free spirit—"

"Admirable!"

"*Oui. Mais . . .* Eugénie is also denied access to her mother whom she is instructed to despise. Although it is true that the mother is a simpering fool, nevertheless, she is made to suffer needlessly and horribly."

"But *why?*"

"Because Franval wants the girl to worship him, to live for him and no one else, to be, in fact, as corrupt as he is himself and as selfish in her pleasures."

"This 'education' is a knife that cuts both ways. She is made into her father's thing!"

"Exactly. The perfect companion for his aesthetic, intellectual, criminal, and sexual delight. Free of moral constraints, 'the pupil of his seductions,' she is totally infatuated with a father she calls 'brother' or 'friend.' *Jamais papa!*"

"Clever bastard."

"There is more. He tells her she is the moving force behind his existence, and this is so. She is the primary project of his life, the mirror of his will. Once he has fucked her, he cannot get enough."

"How hideous this all is! And to what purpose?"

"When he was first sent to prison, Sade wrote an encyclopedic novel of debauchery, which lost when the Bastille was taken." (It's true. *Hélas!* My beloved *120*

*Days . . .* !) "But I got to see a few chapters, and if I respond-
ed at first with outrage, I then considered that all the excesses Sade described were no more nor less than *an illustration of
the idea of slavery taken to its logical conclusion.*"

"I would agree. Slavery is the primary cause of debauchery. Yet what is his object here?"

"To demonstrate that Nature knows no Moral Order.
Nature doesn't give a fig for social conventions or ethical
questions. And God cannot respond to or repair evil, because
He is not there to witness it. But, as I said, the tale roils with
complexities. Just as a child can be ruined by the stupidities
and abject cruelties of religious training, which blunts the
body, the spirit, and the mind, so may the child be corrupted
by a 'cruel, base, and self-serving father'—which is exactly
how Sade describes Franval."

"How does the monster take his daughter?" Olympe asks.
"Does he rape her?"

"There is no need! Simply: He seduces her brilliantly, with
great delicacy and false talk of real choices. Then, in a room
gorged with flowers and upon a throne of fragrant roses, fucks
her."

"Clever, *clever* bastard! And a coward, too!"

"And because she is the perfect mirror of his own passions
and convictions, he falls madly and—as it turns out—fatally
in love."

"I see: Franval is like Narcissus! But why has the mother
allowed it?"

"She, too, is a figment, the product of our age: passive, self-punishing, her mind rotten with ecclesiastical idiocies, her blood watered down with sentimentality. Sade calls her a 'tender soul,' but with irony. She is in truth a passionless, pitiful soul, who, rather than fight for her daughter, wallows in self-pity."

"I don't know which of the two I hate more!"

"Nor I. Together they have produced a monster."

"This Sade of yours is ruled by rage: a Cathar's rage!"

"Exactly so! And here's the proof: When Franval decides Eugénie will not marry and expresses his hatred of marriage to his wife, she asks: 'Then you think the human race should be allowed to die out?' And he replies: 'Why not? A planet whose only product is poison cannot perish too quickly.' "

"These ideas are fascinating and stimulating. It is clear that Franval has, by reducing the child to a thing, poisoned both his world and hers. It follows that he could only long for annihilation."

"That is so! Franval, like his wife, is self-punishing. Sade writes: 'Such was his nature that when he was disturbed, deeply troubled, and wanting to regain peace of mind at any cost, he would obtain it by those means most likely to make him lose it again.' "

"A brilliant study of character!"

"One last thing. Sade demonstrates how Franval has reduced his daughter to an object of his will in this way: His friend Valmont insists on sharing his pleasures. Franval refuses but offers to exhibit Eugénie on a pedestal. He dresses her like a 'savage' and surrounds her with a moat. Her pose is salacious; she stands very still. Valmont is provided with a silk cord. When pulled, it causes her to turn, thus revealing her charms."

"Dear creature," Olympe says, taking both Gabrielle's hands and standing, "let us prove Sade wrong. If the world is plagued with poison, it is also replete with tenderness. I must admit Sade's philosophical tale has warmed me."

About the neck, between her breasts, Olympe wears a little silver amulet the size of a child's thumb and in the shape of a cunt. When Gabrielle sees it, she takes it up in her fingers and laughs.

Olympe says: "Such things were worn during the Renaissance to attract the Evil Eye. Like a venomous snake that strikes with mortal consequence but once within the hour, so the Eye strikes this amulet and thereafter can do no harm. But that is not why I wear it."

"And why do you wear it?" Gabrielle asks, tracing an itinerary across her friend's breasts to tease her desire.

"To proclaim my infatuation with pleasure! And to honor that great dreamer Savinien de Cyrano de Bergerac, who imagined that the moon was inhabited by naked giants wearing bronze phalli at their belts—their only article of dress—instead of daggers! 'Luckless is that country in which the symbols of procreation are held in horror!' he wrote, 'while the agents of destruction are revered!' "

"Ah!" Gabrielle sighs, "where is Savinien now that we so desperately need him? For I fear that the Unique Event in which we are actors shall be rent asunder by the blade."

"A revolution that would sever the brain from the body is one that fears the imagination. Nevertheless, my own imagination is in this instant much aroused." Olympe eases the combs from Gabrielle's hair, and the blouse from her shoulders. . . .

*If for a moment I cease writing my letter to you* [Gabrielle writes], *I hear . . . it is as though I hear the passage of time, mon ami; it is a melancholy singing. And yet—and how strange it is—harmonious. I cannot tell you how sweet it is to recall for you tonight that delightful evening—and how sad!*

*Olympe's raven hair. Her amulet. So vivid that I can, eyes closed, reach out now and seize her wrist, touch the fine veins branching there delicately, like the veins of some strange leaf. The leaf of a rose from some other world.*

*That night, Paris was blanketed with snow. We fell into bed, and it seemed to me in her embrace that the night fanned out in all directions, that we traveled to Otahití and returned, that we bought a universe with glass beads and brass amulets, and gave it back again.*

*"What causes it to snow?" Olympe murmured sometime in the middle of the night.*

*"It is formed of vapors freezing."*

"Every sort of meteor appeals to me," she whispered. "But snow most of all."

"I wish to review your dictations," I told her. "I am one of those rare creatures of the Third Estate who was educated by her father. And we shall read the great minds of our age together, and copy down the phrases that appeal to you the most. You shall put them to memory, learn to punctuate and to spell. In six months you shall be schooled—or so is my intention—and the ink with which you write shall be none other than your own."

"Starlight is the ink I wish," she said, taking my hand in the dark. "The vivacity and clarity of moonlight."

"And what color is this cosmic ink?" I asked her.

"The color of humanity," replied Olympe de Gouges.

## THREE

*A fan-maker,* Restif wrote in a pamphlet he made certain got into the hands of the Comité, *continues not only to ply her frivolous trade, to pander to fops, and to grow plump on the purses and affections of traitors, but, what is worse, to comply with the demands of that beached whale the Marquis de S. . . . whose deliriums cannot be contained by towers, nor by the threat of death, but which, just as certain pernicious growths flourish in the damp of bogs far from the sun and air, fill the atmosphere of Paris with a stubborn stench. . . .*

And so on. And so forth. Thus we are described: you a fraternizer and I a toad with colors—part whale, part poison mushroom, and, like Abraxas, lethal and ridiculous all in the same breath. So monstrous, in fact, that to do as you did, dear vanished friend, to send me books, to write me letters, to, on occasion, visit me with a basket of strawberries or a boxed cake, was enough to seal your fate. Ah! Gabrielle! How could we have known the profundity of Restif's envy, the *toxicité* of his venom?

Now that both you and Olympe are gone: *Is he content?* Has his spirit calmed? Does he inhale the evening air with greater satisfaction? Does he ease himself upon the piss pot with an unequaled groan of *volupté*? Does he, this hour, as I honor your passing with ink and tears, sit by the window of the Café de Chartres (you know the one: the pretty little café at the corner of Rue de Montpensier—I wonder if it is still there!) and gaze out at the faces of the world's prettiest and most intriguing creatures, rosy with the cold of winter? Does he, as he sips his chocolate—lucky bastard!—plot the murder of a *député*—Camille, perhaps—having been so successful with heads of lesser value? (Yes! Yes! I *know:* He doesn't like to *watch.* Yet, as do all the rest, he believes in, *venerates,* the machine!)

Does he—for it is dinnertime—take out his knife, just as I have taken up my pen, to slice into the roast he shares with a member of the Comité de Surveillance? Or does he, as is his habit, indulge in the dark melancholy his murderous zeal does little to alleviate and much to aggravate? Surrounded by the familiar buzz and hum of Paris, chewing his chop, Restif, sipping his bourgogne, stuffing his face with pie, is glum. Why? Because Sade remains. *Sade remains!*

*Are towers to keep assassins safe? Are we waiting for a bigger, a better blade to sever a head so engorged with candy and fever dreams it will take a bullock and a hay cart to carry it away? A risky business,* Restif rages: *As long as Sade's head sits steady on the bloated neck, its astronomical wheels will keep on spinning, bombarding the world with lies, insane seductions, books the Devil himself would be hard-pressed to read. . . .*

"I, for one, will not sleep," says Restif, sucking on a particularly succulent bone, "until Sade is entertaining the flies and their maggots."

His friend agrees: "Sodomites are to France what the pox is to the maid."

"Ah!" Restif smiles companionably. The crackling on his piece of pork is as brown as it is thick, and he is gnawing on it thoughtfully, as grease collects on his chin. "Ah! Sade's time will come!"

"For the moment we have, uh . . . *misplaced him,*" Restif's companion admits (and could it be that maniac Hébert, Robespierre's henchman? The light is dim . . . I can't quite make him out). "But—"

"Misplaced Sade? How is this possible? A man the size of a house? With piles so fulgurant that night turns to day when he drops his drawers? Sade? *Misplaced?*" Hébert, if it is he, pales with shame. Restif is outraged . . . and it is true! They've lost track of me!

Hébert stabs a roasted potato with his fork and, as he salts it, says: "Do not forget, citizen: The jails are full! A third of

Paris is behind bars, or is about to be. It is impossible to keep track of everyone! Just this week, a most fuckable tart named Rose Martin was beheaded by mistake—"

"By mistake!"

"She was mistaken for a dreadful scold named Rose-Marie Martinet!" He roars with laughter. "It happens all the time. But not to worry. When, last week, we rounded up twelve peasants all named Teston and didn't know which of them had made the scene in the street—cursing Sanson and Robespierre so loudly an entire quarter complained of the noise—we cut them down, one and all. As it turned out, our man was dead already! His liver had abandoned him on Rue St-Denis. But so what? In France, hayseeds grow thick as weeds."

"It is true—"

"Perhaps the next crop will be less stupid."

"That's doubtful!"

"Well, then! We agree! These small abuses are inevitable. What matters is this: blood. The gears of the Revolution must be well oiled with it!"

"You can't make a *civet de lièvre* without killing a hare—"

"You can't make a *pâté de foie gras* without killing a goose—"

"You can't make wine without bleeding the grapes!"

"And you can't fuck a whore without unbuttoning your pants!"

⌒

IT IS TRUE that I am envious of Restif's idle conversations, his suppers with friends, his nightly roaming, the fact that he can, at whim, ogle the merry youths roaring their joy in life like lions, the pretty candle-sellers dressed like fairies in grass green, the valets staggering under the weight of turkeys as they speed to some great table, the rouged bosoms of countesses true and false (Ah! but they are a thing of the past; I am forgetting . . .). I envy him because he is at liberty to lap up the displays of rarities in St-Germain, admire the delicious figures of wax that gaze upon the living with such affecting mystery one is drawn to them as to a breathing soul.

Once I fell madly in love with one of these: a serene blonde with pale green eyes of glass and hands as small as moths. She was standing among precious articles: Venetian mirrors, rare porcelains . . . she made me forget that my rooms were already cluttered and could not hold one more thing. I entered the shop and, leaning into the window, touched her hair. It was real! Some milliner or laundress had sold her hair to buy bread, and now it tumbled to the shoulders of a counterfeit girl who so aroused my hunger for beauty that my soul was dazzled!

Gabrielle . . . How I long to touch something beautiful tonight, if only for a moment. Your face, a new pair of kid gloves the color of fresh snow, a silk fan shot with gold! Now that you are gone, who will bring me the first rose of summer, the little cakes I love? With whom shall I share my dreams? Whose letters perfumed with a maddening mix of varnish, rosewater, and rabbit-skin glue will enable me to overcome my nightly terrors? I fear our book will suffer without your lively touch. I fear that without your sweetness to temper my bile, the book will become too dark, too overwrought, too cruel!

My fire is going out, and before I can continue, I must get it going, else freeze. The stove is difficult to manage, as the authorities fear I might brain a guard with a shovel, or shove a poker down his throat. It is fortunate that I have always kept a warming pan for my bed and my stoneware hot-water bottle. These, too, could be used to brain a public servant. To the fire, then, and I'll roast an onion. In prison, the plate is never changed after the soup! (And the soup is execrable, although there is nothing simpler than the making of a good soup!) The potato isn't French but one of those curious vegetables from the New World. Is this why they persist in boiling up weeviled barley? A potato! Something green! A plate of peas with a little pepper, some Normandy butter, a garnish of chopped parsley—and I would be in Paradise, if *mal vêtu* and too ill-equipped to entertain. (I fear they'll outlaw the potato and finish off Parmentier, just as they did Lavoisier; they'll outlaw the oyster for being obscene! Haven't they beheaded the oyster-sellers? And hatters, moralists, actresses, bishops, watch-makers, professors, ice-cream sellers—they will outlaw ice cream! They say du Barry flailed about like a fish—just one of the Revolution's many miracles: *the multiplication of fish.*)

Sometimes, when I am not at my best, but frankly madder than sane, I do a little jig I call "the Saint Guillotine"; my jig is of the sort hens do in all the barnyards of France come Easter. To be authentic, I'd have to do it headless; however, thus far I appreciate my jig's *inauthenticity.*

I'VE HAD MY supper, such as it was. Things could be worse: I can still pay for kindling, an onion, an apple (although the apple was as wrinkled and bruised as the clitoris of an old whore). What I would do for the cutlet I doubt I could digest, some chicken soup well-seasoned with saffron! For the truth of the matter follows: If I have alienated the entire universe by imagining fictive banquets during which little girls, roasted to a turn, are brought steaming to table, I am in point of fact *no cannibal.* Nor am I, nor have I ever been, a *coprophage.* Unlike, I must add, certain saints beloved of the Church whose appetites—for shit, for vomit, for pus and menstrues—have inspired my most feared and hated works. The one thing I once had (for these days, to tell the truth, I dream only of tenderness) in common with the saints was a healthy taste for the whip.

But now having supped, having survived another day, what am I to do to make it through the night? Fortunately,

I've managed over the years to hold on to the dildo of *palissandre*. I call him La Jeunesse, for like a trusted servant I once had, he is always green. (You see how I am reduced to a curé's piteous pleasures.) The other dildos: La Merluche and La Terreur were lost the last time my room was searched for "pornography." (They have stolen more than two dozen manuscripts, including those lost when I was so precipitously removed from the Bastille on the fourteenth of July, 1789; all those my wife destroyed because she feared they would "come into the wrong hands and *compromise me*" [!]; all those I have not been able to hide—for although I keep on my toes, in a manner of speaking, the devils descend like the wind at a moment's notice to sweep up everything in their path. If anything survives, it will be miraculous.)

So, yes, I have La Jeunesse. Ah! *Mais*—it's not that simple. Physical needs are one thing, the needs of the spirit, another. (Note that I did not say "soul" but "spirit.") The spirit must be fed, else it shrivels up too. Well, here is what I do: I reconstruct the city of Paris in my mind. My city opens before me like the buttered ass of an eager hussy, and I am free and I am king. "King?" you say. *"King?" Mais oui!* For here's the thing: In the mind's revolution, each man is king. Who in his right mind would choose to imagine himself a vegetable-peeler?

~

# FOUR

The first thing I do is to give Paris back her ornaments—that is to say, her signs, which were outlawed thirty years ago by that prick Sartines. He resented their size, unbridled paganism, ribaldry, and subversive humor (for there were caricatures of the clergy—wonderfully cruel—and pictures of kings being buggered by bankers). "Paris," said Sartines, "chokes on obscenity." It is true that the signs had proliferated to a dizzying degree, and they had succumbed to gigantism; it seemed the domestic articles of Brobdingnag were hanging everywhere. This proliferation was extreme, and yet in those riotous streets I remember so well, streets in which one needed to duck one's head constantly else be brained by brass roosters, one walked turn by turn entranced, instructed, and amused: intoxicated!

In those days, one read Paris like a book. Imagine Diderot's Encyclopedia thus: Universally Intelligible! An entire education was there or, closer to the truth, potentially so. In other words, I like to imagine my Paris hung not only with pork hocks and wheels of cheese but—and why not?—with the lost phallus of Osiris! The sacred cats of Egypt! Apis and the gemmed bees of Childeric! Here: Perseus holds the Medusa by her hissing hair! There: Diana, buttocks alert, stands beside the plumed Serpent of the Mexicas! Above: Saint Frances's tongue, and, farther down the street: the Holy Mother's Immaculate Cunt!

Speaking of Isis: I give Paris back to her. By hanging her image not only above every corset shop and dairy, but at the place where Gabrielle spent her infancy. In the shadow of St-Germain-des-Prés, I build her a temple, just as it was a few centuries ago, and as it had been since the Devil knows when. Black Isis, Queen of Egypt—I give Paris back to you!

But wait! I am not quite finished hanging signs. If my city is to be instructive, it needs minerals and maps, examples of geological turbulences, body parts, botanical models, bestiaries, and more: throughout the city, accumulations of disparate things wired together and designating the public wonder rooms where a multiplicity of possible orderings of Nature would teach Rational Thought and, thus, *Skepticism*.

Having imagined the signs, the inns (Le Con d'Or, La Bite d'Argent, Le Cul Royal, La Mandragore), the gardens (the Garden of Helpless Love, of Jealous Love, of Illicit Love, of

Impossible Pleasures, of Memory, of Ideal Encounters, of Pandemonium, and of Promise), the whores (Séminale, Boulimia, Pomona, Féline, Sucette . . .), I next imagine a calendar of days:

A day devoted to memory; an entire month devoted to the study of dreams; a festival in honor of the prostate, of seminal fluid, of the orgasm; the opening of an academy devoted to the erogenous zones; a day to honor the Dog Star, the equinoxes and solstices; a month to honor astronomy and all the planetary and stellar phenomena; a surgeon's day; a day to honor pastry chefs (with prizes given to those most adept in the manufacture of puff pastry); a day devoted to the public mourning of Life's Errors; an entire year given over to the study of Primary Causes; a day devoted to International Forums on Masturbation; a day taken up with the fabrication of *grimoires* of chocolate; a month to honor Architecture, vanilla, and the coffee bean; a day in which everyone will wear a Persian bonnet and make beer; a day to honor mollusks and polenta; an entire year devoted to roses, another to lilies, another to irises, another to the phallus, the cunt, and gingerbread; an entire century to celebrate the Death of God; an entire century to condemn Bad Faith, the notion of God's Grace, the Guillotine, the Pillory, the hangman's noose, and English cookery; a decade devoted to perfume.

Saturdays: turned over to the painting and repair of all buildings public and private—everyone in work clothes, damsels with brooms, lots of fucking in municipal rooms; and in the evening: bonfires, pig roasts, carnival comedies.

Sundays: a public scrubbing—all assholes good as new; free dental work and lessons in the morality of Amorous Strategy, the precepts of an Enlightened Atheism, the Erotic Arts, and Philosophical Inquiry. Free theater, bouquets of seasonal flowers, and novels offered all around; cannons melted down into goblets, water pipes, and cowbells; midnight balls and—in the Maya manner—barbecues.

Monday through Friday: days officiated by a *Papa Fatuatum*—a Pope of Fools—to be elected each week. (All this as just another way of spitting in the eye of Saint-Just, who would have everyone a farmer, a soldier, or a worker—no fancies, no delights, *no women!* No fucking, no buggery, no sauces, candy, theater, books: just dull-witted eunuchs all dressed in canvas and horse hair and all made to sleep *like cattle on the floor!*)

In my Paris, everyone has a bed, a big beautiful bed with curtains of calico (summer) and velvet (winter) and sheets as white as cream! These beds to be the sanctuaries of erotic experiment, clarity, and amorous confusion.

In my Paris, *drôles* and *drôlesses* are so disguised as to have abandoned their particular humanity for a unique *transparency* of being. In other words: They are so *visible* in their disguises that they can no longer be seen. They bounce off the eye as a rubber ball bounces off the playing field. Wherever they walk, the city is a stage—a constant parade of true inventions! Fashion as the epitome of chaos! On stilts, in slippers of green glass, in pewter suits, in wigs of lilies . . . I dress my Paris in the hues not of convention, but of my own invention: fresh pea-porridge green, a deep violet called "Neptune's balls," rose the color of the palms of a Nigerian princess, a brassy gold called "Giulio Romano." There are two rules only, and here they are:

1. *All ecclesiastical categories must be resolutely pagan or satirical.*
2. NOTHING WILL EVER RECUR.

High Priests of Astonishment, Masters and Mistresses of Masturbatory Madness, the Hierophants of the Sexual Heart, the Earls of Ejaculation—all roll into town on Thursdays in shoes fitted out with wheels. They are dressed in the manner of Mozabites; they wear masks of silk and silk veils; only their sex—always prodigious—is visible. Their task is to animate and imagine the Public Peep Shows wherein one may see a naked Perseus sporting a stony phallus and approaching the Gorgon with horror and admiration, or simply watch a maiden sweetly sleeping, a flight of geese (now, there's a thing of such sumptuous banality it makes me weep just to think of it!), a cat licking her paws, a fishwife fucking an eel, a child eating a waffle, a field of wild lilies, a forest stream, a meadow brook, the sky, the sea . . .

This is what dreaming my Paris has taught me: that an infinite number of cities are possible; that our Revolution could have moved bloodlessly, with imagination and grace; that instead of burning, my Paris might have blossomed.

LAST NIGHT I dreamed of my enemy Restif. Because of my girth, I was sleeping on my back, although it is said that this is unhealthy. I had pulled the bed curtains as close as I could to my body because of the intense cold, and the blankets—so threadbare they will have to be replaced sometime soon, but when? . . . the blankets I had pulled up to my nose.

In my dream, Restif and I were walking toward the Maubée fountain among trollops tricked out in the feathers of pheasants and swans. Each one wore a red ribbon tied to her neck "to keep our heads where they belong!" (This shouted from the street by a strapping redhead who saw how we both stared.) Then all the whores laughed bitterly and *cautiously* together.

We continued on. In the back of my mind I knew that Restif, although he was being companionable, was taking "the long way" to my execution. In the Faubourg-St-Martin, men moved like ghosts in the deserted streets, pushing wheelbarrows filled with human heads shorn of hair—a detail that struck me as particularly ominous as well as queer. . . . We found ourselves next crossing Rue St-Honoré by way of Les Poulies, where the blood of the slain had puddled. Someone had set down a makeshift bridge of planks, and we stepped across it gingerly. "Some stew of tripe!" Restif exclaimed. "Bah!" (He had soiled his shoes.)

Then we were in St-Germain, and there came upon a throng of masons, carpenters, and the wives of executioners trafficking in the clothes of corpses and other nasty things; and also grooms, gold-beaters, doctors with their needle boxes and medicine bottles hanging from their headless necks; knife-sellers and salt-sellers. All were walking toward the Luxembourg gardens and holding their heads in their hands. In the cafés, the servers stood by looking dazed as their clients streamed past—clients who, had they wanted a glass of wine, could not have ordered it, nor drunk it down. "Business could be better," a girl sighed as we passed, adjusting the ribbon at her neck with trembling fingers. "I've not poured a drink all morning!"

The gardens had been torn apart to make room for the graves; everywhere the earth heaved with the dead or was deeply pitted with holes. The stench was untenable . . . and the noise! For the place swarmed with criers carrying shovels and shouting out the names of those sentenced:

"Bernadette Fossour!"
"Thomas Clippet!"
"Reine Latour!"
"Martin Gueux!"

One by one the dead leapt into the waiting graves, holding their heads and, as though they were playing a game,
shouting:

"*Et hop!*" And "*Hop-là! Hop! Hop! Hop!*"

"You hear that?" I said, turning to Restif. "They've not
called my name."

"But they shall!" he beamed. "Without a doubt!"

Then all was submerged by a tide of bleating sheep, driv-
en by shepherds who, above the tumult, shouted:

"The dead, too, must eat!"

"Since when are the needs of the dead of interest to the
living?" Restif snorted disdainfully.

The scene changed. We were in an open field. Exhausted,
we spied a haystack and thought it a fine place to sleep.
Drawing closer, I saw it was made not of hay but of hair; in
any case, I did not want to spend the night in such close quar-
ters with Restif. Leaving him there, I continued on alone
until I came to a field of blue lupines. Stretching out among
them, I awoke from my dream, having torn both blankets and
ripped the curtains from their hooks!

I awoke to a terrific hubbub: the sound of hammering and
shouting. For one joyous instant I thought: *They are taking
down the guillotine at last!*

"It is the Festival of Reason!" the dullard who brings me
my water each day informed me—having, as usual, spilled
most of it before unlocking the door. "They say there's people

screwing on the altar in Notre-Dame! A regular orgy in the
sacristy! A cobbler named Clootz pissed into the face of Jesus
Christ!"

"And *down there*?" I asked, peering out the window and
into the courtyard, where the guillotine still loomed but
where a platform was under construction. A crowd had gathered to watch men in britches the color of dung carry a crude
statue as ugly as sin: "What the fuck is going on *down there*?"

"Reason Herself!" the wine-sop sputtered with excitement. He put down the pitcher with such ill-advised force
that it cracked. "She's to stand beside the chopper—" Indeed,
as he spoke the thing was hoisted up and set to stand beside
the block.

"The view," I sighed, "is not much improved." This *bon mot*
caused the scoundrel to kick over my pitcher in a fit of temper. It shattered, and as he refused to bring me another I am
forced to spend the day *without water*. To freshen my face I
rubbed it with a little brandy I keep for head colds, but the
nitwit left the chamber pot and I am forced to breathe that
essence of man as I sit here, attempting to gather the shreds of
myself about me, and this despite the racket.

Ten will be executed today in Reason's name: a most
unreasonable number.

So! The day dawns under the sign of the Broken Pitcher
and the Full Chamber Pot. It is likely that the afternoon will
unfold under the sign of Shadow. Already darkness, palpable,

thick as treacle, enters into my body's every orifice. Shadow is the primary sign and lesson of the times and the place; *malgré moi* I am a student of Applied Darkness.

THERE ARE THOSE born under the sign of Revolt; others under the sign I call the Maze; others, born under Charybdis, are designated by a vortex of gravel and ice. Good days—those animated by the sun, the ocelot, the water lily—when the mind heats up like a meteor and I, dizzy with the speed of the fall, cling to my pen (the one thing that grounds me)—I write. I write a storm of such power it annihilates everything else. Restif is right: My tower cannot contain it, and already it rages through the world. It sets the world on edge; it tips the balance of things. This storm is called Juliette, when it is not called *Justine.*

~

# FIVE

*Sade—you once said to me: "Living in a cell is like suckling a sword." So it is for me tonight. If I lift my eyes from this letter for an instant only, I taste blood. But looking down, dipping my quill in this precious ink, the past resurges and I am far from this unforgiving place. . . .*

Thus Gabrielle continued her letter to me that last night. And, a thing marvelous in itself, as I read her letter I, too, travel back in time and space and am far, far away. The next morning, after their first amorous encounter, Gabrielle returned alone to the *atelier* in time to meet a party of Turks,

*all wanting some very sumptuous fans "depicting those delicious pleasures that decency keeps us from naming and that you"—each man prettily inclined his turbaned head—"execute with such delicacy. . . ." I showed them all we had. Their eyes were so hot I feared the fans would catch fire! But in the end, they requested new scenes from me. My female figures were not fat or pink enough! These swarthy men with raven beards were after blondes in the Flemish mode, rollicking in "exotic" interiors—that is to say, French gazebos and boudoirs well provided with bolsters and hassocks. In accordance with their taste, La Fentine, particularly fetching in striped cotton, made for us all coffee well flavored with cardamom, in the Turkish manner. We nibbled* beignets *from across the way—the ones you love (and who will get them to you now?)—dusted with sugar and flavored with orange-blossom water. The* beignets, *the coffee, the liberty with which Frenchwomen disport themselves, all conspired to prompt the handsomest of the group to invent these lines in our honor:*

> *O keeper of delight,*
> *May these ladies' nights,*
> *Transpire beneath starry skies:*
> *Pleasure them, Allah,*
> *Until they die.*

*These lines were supposedly intended for the three of us, yet were clearly inspired by La Fentine. Indeed, later in the day a gown of* framboise *and gold* brocart *arrived for her along with a card signed simply: "A Meanderer." "This," I told her, "means he comes from the Meander River valley. I*

remember my father once pointed to it on an old and brightly
colored map." La Fentine wanted to see the map but hélas, it
had been lost when Father's shop was burned. That a man
might in his life take a winding course, as does a river, evoked
something deep within her. All day La Fentine was silent—a
thing wondrous in itself! When a small, beautifully wrought
box of brass arrived the next day containing a solitary gem—a
black pearl the size of an eye—I knew La Fentine would be
leaving soon and did my best to prepare my heart against her
absence. Four thousand fan-makers in Paris—but none as
gifted as she. (As it turned out, business was slow and I did
not replace her. I did not do badly—so many were out of
work: the gauze- and lace-makers especially. The Revolution
despises frivolity, as you know; more than one lace-maker is
forced to fuck if she would eat!)

The pearl had been set in silver. That afternoon, I put aside
my paints and brushes to make for her a choker of braided ribbon the colors of silver old and new, with one solitary framboise thread running through. When La Fentine's Meanderer
reappeared with an invitation to dinner, she was ready. Tall
and dark, slender as a reed, her breasts no bigger than plums,
there was nothing "Flemish" about her! And yet . . . Her
suitor had seen that she was a treasure house of tender pleasures. The night he came for her, La Fentine shimmered!

Not long after, they married in Neuilly—in Monsieur de
Saint-James's eccentric garden. It was November. Well bundled
up against the cold, the party drank to the couple's health

under trees hung with balls of yellow glass. We supped in an artificial grotto made into a fanciful arbor with the bones of fish, and heated with brass braziers as in Roman times. Monsieur de Saint-James, a collector of everything from fountains to the skins of snakes, was a feverish soul, harmless yet clearly mad. He pointed out the various species of fish whose skeletons had provided the canopy: the ribs of whales, the spines of eels . . . the entire ceiling was constellated with starfish. (I have heard that these marvels were destroyed last summer, rather than saved for everyone's delight. Yet it is foolish to mourn the passing of a fancy—no matter how charming—in times such as these.)

"I very much hope that Turkish wives are better treated than French ones," Olympe sighed once La Fentine had been swept away by her Meanderer. "After all, in France marriage is said to be menaced by lasciveté and not enhanced! The wife who makes her marriage a place of pleasure acquires in the public eye the attributes of the courtesan. Her husband distrusts her. The better a wife in bed, the greater a husband's jealousy." It is true! That very week, a fan-maker of my acquaintance had lost an eye to her husband's anger!

We were exploring the garden alone; Monsieur de Saint-James had made us a map of his marvels—among them, cascades of warm water covered with glass.

"How frivolous this is!" Olympe suddenly declared. "There is a fine line between the frivolous and the marvelous, and here our host has crossed it!"

"It is true," I said, taking her hand, "that since the Greeks, pleasure has always taken place outside of marriage."

"A tradition to uphold," she laughed, nibbling my fingers one by one.

"The Greek wife labored in the garden growing domesticated plants. These exemplified her husband's seed," said I, "and her own fecundity."

"How dull! And the whore? Tell me about the whores of Greece! What were their gardens like?"

"They had no time to garden! But exemplified wildness and the heady perfumes of savage things. Rosemary growing in crags, and thyme and sage beside the mountain paths. Brushing against these plants, the clothes are perfumed—as is the lover who embraces them. 'Hour after hour,' one poet said, 'you are haunted by the smell of their wildness!' "

"As when I first saw you," she said. "I left the atelier and took your fragrance home with me. Waiting for you, I was so agitated by the persistence of your perfume my hands shook! You smell of rosemary," she said. "Fan-maker, you smell of illicit delight." Then she put her arms about me and I could feel her heart leaping beneath her cloak. "I don't give a fig if Restif calls me a débauchée impudique and puts me on his short list of current whores!" she whispered in my ear.

I laughed: "Let us counter his list of whores with a list of bores."

"It will be a long one!" said she.

༄

TWO THINGS, DEAR Sade, you must know: In September, when Olympe applied to her section's Comité de Surveillance for a "good-citizenship certificate," she was refused. Or rather, the scoundrel in charge, a pig named Bouhélier, cited Restif's list of whores.

"Show me your cunt," he said. "Then, perhaps, if I find it to my liking, I'll give you a certificate, madame, and mes hommages!" (I should say that I never applied for one myself. It seems an indignity and an absurdity. Besides—the things are bought and sold like salty rolls! And furthermore: If women cannot vote, nor meet together, they cannot be called citizens!)

The month after La Fentine's wedding, Olympe's play L'Esclavage des Noirs was performed by the Comédie-Française—and this despite the ominous "weather."

In the first place, the actresses had quarreled over the part of the slave, Mirza, until they realized that she was to be played black. Then no one wanted the part. Next, the colons, many in retirement in Paris, having pressured the maréchal to postpone the play for three years, were enraged to discover it had been scheduled. Further: When the actors who were to play slaves realized that Olympe expected them all to be black, they got a lettre de cachet against her. Fortunately the judge called the affair ridiculous, or she might have landed in jail.

"*The theater is a lesson in Virtue and Tolerance,*" Olympe told the actors at the first rehearsal. "*No wonder Voltaire called the Comédie-Française a 'puppet theater'! You are all puppets of the* colons*!*" Taking great strides across the stage as the actors cringed, she raged:

"*All my life I have been harried by those who would intimidate me. Penniless, without education, I have paid for my current freedom with humiliations beyond number. But I am a writer,* mes amis, *not a criminal, nor an hysteric to be muzzled and leashed! My play is not a wall to be white-washed at will!*

"*All my life,*" she hissed, surrounded by the actors, who, silenced, seemed to be listening, "*I have turned a deaf ear to interdictions and decrees. The words 'compulsory' and 'required' disgust me, as do words of so-called advice, good counsel from fools, fleas in the ear!*"

Hélas—she had not shamed or inspired them, but enraged them. "*We will not be Negroes!*" they cried.

Here is how it turned out. The actors played their parts as "*savages*" from an imaginary continent, in grass skirts, turbans, and nose rings—and all were heavily rouged. But it was impossible to know if the play was as bad as people have said, for the colons came each and every one to pound the floor with their canes and, without pause, shout violences and obscenities. The madman Hébert screamed "*Kill them all!*" at the top of his lungs, although it was unclear whom he wanted *dead. Robespierre left as soon as the shouting began; Danton, looking nauseous, attempted to still the crowd to no avail; the great actress Montansier was busy kissing a young officer named Bonaparte; and a group of mulattoes from San Domingo, who had come to Paris to assert their rights before the National Assembly, sat as still as faience.*

*Restif was there, and his broadside hit the streets the very next day:*

I have been called a pornographer. It is true that I am. I use the word "lightly"! My pen is clean, straightforward, and brisk. I am no fop, nor am I a libertine. It is one thing to extol a virile sexuality and another to trumpet bum-fucking—as does a certain marquis, or murderer—as does a certain Olympe de Gouges. You see: I do not mince my words!

To the despair of clean-living citizens, the collapse of morals is everywhere in evidence. I have elsewhere described the brazen effeminates—ten times more provocative than any harlot, their big feet dissimulated by high-heeled slippers—causing commotion in the cafés. Yet such sights could not prepare me for what I have just seen: a play, performed in our own National Theater, calling for the death of French colonials at the hands of their servants, a play written by a woman who would be a man, performed by

actors against their own will and better judgment for
an audience better suited for harvesting sugarcane!

There is more: The marriage of a certain fan-
maker's assistant took place in Neuilly last month. I
had been told that this beauty—a bastard who had for
years lived in the streets—was to marry a Turkish
prince! The story amused me; I managed to inform
myself as to the particulars and to slip onto the property without being seen. There I saw Olympe de
Gouges, also in the bushes, embracing the fan-maker
with an *empressement* to make a Turk blush! I left hur-
riedly to pen everything down while still fresh, thinking I might have been in Italy!

On my way home I was nearly knocked silly by a
large marrowbone tossed from a window and into
the street. I spent the evening in bed with a fresh cabbage leaf dressing the top of my head.


Restif a pornographer? Bah! He is not worthy of the
name. Pornography is Satan's seat: the place of eternal spon-
taneous combustion. Pornography is Hell's capitol, hermeti-
cally sealed, impenetrable, and impassable. A place so corrupt
that it is in fact an embolus in the body of Nature. A place of
such acute congestion and stagnation that within its bound-
aries, time and space are clotted together and stilled. *La lenteur*
is pornography's primary characteristic, *la lenteur* and all the

universe's weight focused on one point. And that point is the conjunction of two bodies: the deliberate body of the pornographer-procrastinator—who is always the violator— and the body of his object, which shorn of will exemplifies the deceleration of the tomb.

Ah. But how weary am I and how sad. It is your letters, Gabrielle, that keep me sane.

> *As you know, dear friend, I matured in poverty. Yet each day unfolded in wonder, and this because of my mother's gypsy ways—how she could from rags make petticoats to tempt a duchess—and because of my father's endless supply of books in all shapes and sizes, and in all manner of disrepair. My books of fairy tales and travels to distant lands were riddled by worms, green with mold, and sometimes blackened and brittle because they had come so close to the fire. . . .*

ᔓ

# SIX

Of those who, like myself, were born beneath the sign of the
Tiger, this is what the Indians of the New World said:

"All bad was his lot; misery befell him. He wallowed in
evil and was covered in filth. Nowhere had he good repute.
He committed adultery, was an adulterer, adulterous . . ."

I HAVE ALWAYS been combustible.

A VERY MANY years ago, a lifetime ago (I was six), I visited
Genzano with that tireless tumble-nun, my uncle the *abbé*. We
traveled by coach and were accompanied by my forlorn but
stoic tutor and the strumpet Pélisse (*poils-aux-cuisses*), who
when she was not stuffing her face with seedcake was on her
knees sucking Uncle's rebounding cock—behind doors, trees,

trellised nooks, confessionals, cemeteries: in other words, whenever we stopped (which we did often). The trip from Saumane to Genzano took forever. The *abbé* de Sade was indefatigable and Pélisse infinitely obliging.

When he was not reading pornography ill-concealed in theological treatises, my uncle was perusing a fantastic book on the Spanish Inquisition in the New World, illustrated with a multitude of copper engravings, a kind of catalogue of sexual terror, licentious extravagance, and murder. As the *abbé* was so often engaged with Pélisse, and as my tutor was on his own knees after some bug or other, or pressing flowers into a book, or mending his own frayed clothes, and as I was left alone in the coach, I had plenty of time to gloat over those instructive scenes that—as was later proved—assured my life would be ruled by *furia amorosa* and an unbridled imagination.

Of all the extraordinary images that book contained, the one that struck me most profoundly, struck me to the core and the marrow, was of a diminutive Indian maiden, hanging naked by her feet, as priests, leering or scowling, held crucifixes to her face, and as a figure in a hood whipped her vulnerable body, which, I could clearly see, was already tigered from bottom to top. Another exemplary image proposed a circle of youths, all neat and tight, buggering one another before an idol upon whose erect phallus burned a little lamp. Wetting my finger with drool and turning the pages with terror and excitement, I came upon another amazing sight:

an iron crucifix heated to incandescence in the dungeon fire and used to brand six youths all chained by their ankles, necks, and wrists to the floor. *Ah!* thought I with a shudder of loathing and dark delight: *Ah! So nothing is forbidden by Nature! All is permitted!* ("All is permitted," the *abbé* de Sade speculated several years later when I broached the subject of his secret library and in particular this one book. "All is permitted in God's name." "There is no God," was my response, "and *that* is why nothing is forbidden." Uncle roared with laughter.)

But back to our Italian voyage. Impervious to the delightful landscapes, the picturesque villages, the sumptuous woodlands, we passed, I, in my sexual impatience and curiosity, could think only of returning to Uncle's castle on the hill, to idle away my hours in his sumptuous library of incendiary books. *No wonder,* thought I, *Uncle's nose is always in a book! His fist busy in his breeches!* And indeed, marvels in vast numbers awaited me. A precocious reader, by the age of eight I had devoured *A History of Flagellants, Saintly Perversions, The Fetish Cults of Africa, Nights in a Turkish Harem, The Mirror of Pleasure, Le Curé et la Drôlesse, Petit Truc, Gros Machin, The Nun Who Ate Her Own Ordure,* and so on.

That night I could not sleep until Pélisse (*poils-au-pubis*) brought me a little glass of anise-seed water to soothe my mind; better still, she gave me *une petite branlette*—my first. This was to be a habit with us thereafter: the water, the *branlette* (not that it amounted to much!).

Even then my tastes were well defined. "Put your finger up my ass!" I told her. "Or I'll tell the *abbé* what a slut you are!"

"Your uncle knows what I am," Pélisse retorted, her eyes flashing. "And you, monsieur le marquis, *are a monster.*"

"If that is so," I replied, made fearless by what I had seen, "I am in good company."

This rebuke so impressed her that she no longer teased me but, instead, looked at me with new interest. She told my uncle that sooner or later I would be "a force to be reckoned with."

"And what sort of 'force' would that be?" We were all together in the carriage; Genzano just visible in the near distance.

"Of *Nature!*" said I without hesitating. "I wish to be a force of Nature."

"Nature! No less!" My uncle the *abbé* roared with laughter. "He wants to be a force of Nature!" He was still laughing as we entered Genzano.

THE NEXT DAY was Corpus Christi. Uncle insisted we eat *simply*—his joke! We ate no meat, it is true, but were served a feast of fish: raviolis stuffed with a *hachis* of crayfish served in a sauce of curried cream; the white, sweet flesh of eels *en croûte;* a salmon *pâté;* and for dessert a hazelnut *soufflé,* the *spécialité* of Genzano. . . . *Ensuite,* a little walk about the square

and then off to bed and the brief ceremony Pélisse had insti-
gated with such generosity.

"Take *ma broquette* into your mouth!" I cried, "just as you
do to Uncle!"

"Fa! I dare not!" said she. "Your morsel is so small, I fear I
might swallow it!"

"It is well attached!" I insisted, giving her the demonstration.

Thus was I indoctrinated in the ways of the world by my
uncle's mistress. Other mistresses awaited at home; the
Château de Saumane was in truth a harem and a bordello
rolled into one, and my uncle's fortune and position a verita-
ble Aladdin's lamp! I was brought up to believe that the priv-
ileges of power were boundless—or, rather, that they were
bounded only by the imagination.

Now I would turn from this conviction with horror, but
until the abuses of power were made so palpable, *beneath my
very nose,* you might say, I lived by the Laws of Vanity and
Excess. Laws written in tears, fuck, and blood. Nothing at this
time would give me greater solace than an affectionate tumble with a compassionate soul!

But I am forgetting: We are still in Genzano. . . .
Sometime before dawn I heard subtle noises from the street
below and awakened for an instant. Smells of flowers and
freshly chopped heather filled the air and wafted into the
room. I fell back into slumber again, only to awaken, perhaps

an hour later, when the streets echoed with cries and the sounds of cart wheels on the cobbles. The air rang with voices: A girl was singing, a boy joined in; I heard laughter, shouts, a joyous clatter. In a dim corner of the room, my tutor slept fitfully, his hands clutching at his own throat as though he might strangle himself in his dreams.

I leapt from bed and, opening the shutters, peered down into the street, where elaborate and exquisite *tableaux* of multicolored flowers were forming with a swift and inspired sorcery before my eyes. These *tableaux* were of the armorial bearings of the local lords, the bishop, and the Holy See; griffins were rampant and lions *couchant* or *passant;* a sidelong-looking leopard was made entirely of purple pansies bedded down in the damp grass. Flittermice, a marigold tiger in a field of red roses, eight crocodiles, eleven lizards, twelve serpents—but no rabbits to be seen anywhere. Sheaves of wheat; chains of gold; one very white ass. I roused my tutor, and soon we were both delighting in the spectacle. Our room gave us a splendid view, and we took breakfast at the window, only later descending with Uncle and Pélisse (*poils au calice*) to join the admirably tricked out crowds and look on as monks, singing their insipid inanities, walked toward the church, trampling the gorgeous blossoms beneath their filthy feet. I was enraged to see the sumptuous images scattered and ruined and, with all the energy I could muster, shouted: "Miserable crows! Stop where you stand! Not a step farther!"

The *abbé* de Sade grabbed my ear and ordered me to remain silent, but such was my rage that it could not be contained.

It was then that the extraordinary happened: A little Italian dressed in a white frock, her head garlanded with white roses, summoning the fairy forces of a small tempest, began to cry out, too: "You are being very *bad*!" she shouted at the monks. "Surely Jesus hates to see you trampling His flowers!" The child imitated my rage exactly. "Miserable crows!" For the briefest instant we shared a burning look of jubilant defiance and complicity. "Boors!" she cried. "Brigands!"

This little scene so amused the *abbé* that he let go my ear and began to laugh. Pélisse joined in, and even my tutor— always so melancholy—smiled. Better still, the little Italian was laughing, as was her blushing and, it must be said, *superbe* mama.

"The children are of the same mind, *signora*," said the *abbé* de Sade to the lady, acknowledging with an admiring look her uniquely seductive qualities. He bowed; she gave him her hand to kiss.

"My little Alessandra is a wild one." She smiled. "I shall need to marry her quickly!"

"I will never marry!" cried the sublime Alessandra, shaking her black curls and tossing me another of her fiery glances. As it turned out, she was nine, a gifted student of the harp and as naughty as she was beautiful. To our delight, her mama's own faith in the Catholic Church had been made both porous and malleable by the full radiance of her charms and a heretical interest in the pagan mysteries. As she and her daughter were to my uncle's taste, we all ended up together in church—a service made palatable by the artifices of music, candles, and a profusion of flowers. Mass over, my uncle suggested dinner. His behavior, as always in the world, was cheerful and courteous beyond reproach; tactfully submerged in a jealous rage, Pélisse was silent and my tutor unusually entertaining. As the adults chatted about the Templars and the Cathars, the best way to stuff a turkey, and the escapades and intrigues that, Alessandra's mama explained, "animated Genzano year-round," I held Alessandra's hand, concealed as it was beneath a voluminous linen napkin.

I recall that we sat on a ruined but glorious balcony with a view of lazy gardens, woodlands, and towers; and that we dined at an emerald-green table.

"The harp is like the heart," Alessandra lisped. Her eyes were the bluest I have ever seen. "Its strings must be handled with delicacy."

You see how I have never forgotten Alessandra, who, stunning at nine, must have been a danger to public safety at nineteen! The very thought of that beauty in full flower is enough—even after all these years!—to make me roar. That afternoon in Genzano, I fell in love. And then, upon our return to France and Uncle's isolated castle, how many nights beneath the blind stars, a captive of those grim stones, did I dream of the flower pictures of Genzano and of the child whose memory, like the memory of a melody, became fainter and fainter with the passing of the years—only to burst into flame for an instant today.

THE DINNER IN Genzano was unforgettable for another reason: It was the first time I ate Gorgonzola! (A minute of silence as I recall the taste of Gorgonzola with ripe blue figs, a fistful of walnuts, fresh bread . . . and now a sip of . . . what shall it be? Yes! *Ligurian* wine.)

I am:

> *combustible,*
> *volcanic,*
> *excitable,*
> *fractious,*
> *perverse;*
> *a hothead,*
> *impatient (if patience is the ladder of the philosophers,*
> > *I am forever the slave of this tower),*
>
> *convulsive,*
> *agitated,*
> *passionate,*
> *BUT I AM NOT MURDEROUS;*
> *of savage intelligence,*
> *of disorderly emotions,*

*I DWELL IN THE BELLY OF THE WIND;*
*of acute mind,*
*animated,*
*enamored of the*
*OPPOSITE EXTREME IN EVERYTHING;*
*easily exhilarated,*
*when despondent, profoundly so,*
*tempestuous;*
*galvanized by a look, an idea, a memory,*
*imprudent,*
*OF CONTRARY DISPOSITION;*
*grotesque (although once of good features, slight and fair);*
*the eternal friend of a fearless and thoughtful woman:*
*GABRIELLE (What is it that I loved best about her?*
   *The fact that she lived equally in the mind, the body,*
   *and the imagination.)*
*I am a man who loves cats (have repeatedly asked to keep*
   *a cat, have repeatedly been refused).*
*A pornographer who has never forgotten the grape-haired*
   *Alessandra, his first love.*
*A libertine who loves the moon as much as he loves the*
   *lantern.*
*An atheist WHO WOULD SPIT IN THE FACE OF*
   *GOD HAD HE THE CHANCE.*
*A MAN WHO THUS FAR HAS NOT BEEN*
   *REDUCED TO GROVELING LIKE AN*
   *ANIMAL.*

*Things I have done:*

—Paid some whores with whom to frolic, such frolic to include flagellation and fellatio. The girls said to be both articulate in and sensible to the language of the broom. I fed them Spanish fly, foolishly putting far too much into the manufacture of the little anise-flavored *diavolini,* causing the creatures—there were four in all—acute distress (this to my chagrin and embarrassment!). All recovered nicely within a few days, but Restif, already my rival, spread the rumor that the whores had been poisoned with arsenic: *murdered by my hand!* This foolishness—the *niaiserie* of overheated youth, and the misguided notion that more of a good thing is better— was just one of the many mistakes I made in my green years, and for which I have paid, and plenteously, through the nose.*

Upon reflection, it seems to me that in a Rational World, whores need to be knowledgeable not only in the handling of brooms, but in the properties of all the aphrodisiacs: Spanish fly, celery, truffles, oysters, and so on; to be versed in both the pharmacy and the kitchen. Thus, in their waning years, they could use this knowledge to acquire a new *métier.* Imagine the inns and pharmacies of France manned by Sluts in Retirement!

---

*In fact, it was not the so-called "poisoning" that condemned me, but the fact that I fucked my valet in the ass before the assembled *manieuses!*

—Paid a trollop, found in the street, to join me in my rooms for a trussing and a thrashing; soothed her stripes with a Salve of my invention, which, as it turned out, PROVED THE CURE, although she swore I'd poured hot wax into wounds I'd inflicted with a knife! When she was made to show her backside to the court physician, he swore it was as smooth as a baby's! Yet Restif (Restif again!) wrote that I had beaten the wench senseless, burned her with a red-hot poker, seared her flesh with hot wax, and—in order to impregnate her—hung her by the ankles!

—Seduced, with my wife's complicity, my sister-in-law, Anne-Prospère de Launay, a canoness (!), as tall as my wife was short, as pretty as she was not, and as reasonable as one could wish; seduced her, to the intense delight of the two of us, my wife's amusement, and my mother-in-law's eternal rage—a rage I can only call cosmical.* Incest and adultery *with a canoness* was a potion too heady to resist, especially with a woman as intelligent as this. One of my fondest memories of my brief moments of liberty is of a time we spent together in Venice—this was '72, I believe—and *Genzano!* There, ennobled by the memory of my first passion, our improbable, impossible, and yet *inevitable* romance flourished. I recall a delirium of animal pleasure: the kisses shared, the crayfish devoured in quantity, the brilliant conversation; how again

*Her rage; Restif's envy, his lies and exaggerations; and the bile of that genderless Robespierre, who carries a poker up his ass at all times, are responsible more than my acts, more than my imaginings, for my eternal imprisonment.

and again I brought her to tears and to pleasure, simultaneously, with a crucifix.

I'VE NEVER HAD the time or the patience for mild or dry
amusements. Hoping to save what was left of his reputation
and to contain my ardor—and assure the *rent,* for he had
squandered everything in *libertinage*—Father set about to
marry me off. He unearthed a collection of relics more or less
rich, more or less handsome. One was a canoness with the
sumptuous name Damas de Fuligny de Rochoir. I heartily
embraced the idea of bum-fucking a canoness, but that fell
through. There was also a Mademoiselle de Bassompierre.
"Old Stony Bottom," I called her, for although we never did
meet it was rumored that her digestion was static, her teeth
made of bone, and her hair not her own. My soldier's reputation had excited her papa—a man with a weakness for
*grenadiers*—but when the rest leaked out—my incessant lubri-
cious ferment, my gambling, and my atheism: yes, above all,
*my atheism!*—*le père* Bassompierre turned and ran.

*Tant mieux!* I wrote Father. France had just lost her slice of
India and America to the crumpet-eaters but still held the
Antilles. I begged him to find me a glorious mulatta for a
bride. *I dream of a blue clitoris!* said I, *and very black eyes!* Father
scolded me for my frivolity. Such a matter would prove cost-
ly and take forever, and he wanted me off his hands *aussi vite
que possible!* At last he found me Renée Pélagie. As plain as
pudding, she had a fat nose and the chin of a cavalryman.

However, her boyishness did not displease me: *Elle avait du chien,* her ass was sublime. I was enchanted by her willingness to fool around, to be *molinized.* In other words, my wife loved to bum-fuck; she was up for anything. Better still, her father housed us in Paris along with a solicitous valet and a wanton chambermaid. Renée's mother found me "lovable" then, even when she got wind of my little escapades.

"*Qu'il est drôle, le petit mari!*" she liked to say. "How he amuses me!" Oh! Life was worth living then! Adulterous canoness Anne! Benevolent buggeress Renée! Money to burn, feasting and carousing: What a noodlehead I have been! Had I spent my life making enema nozzles instead of ejaculating and book-writing, why, I'd be asleep in the arms of a loving wife. Yet the ardent water that flows in my veins, if calmed, is not stilled. Only Death—

"WHAT IS BELOW is like what is above, and what is above is like what is below." Except *tighter.*

BACK TO PHARMACEUTICALS: Because my pleasure has always depended on displeasure—including my own—and in my attempt to mitigate the *dégâts,* as it were, I investigated various herbs, unguents, and devices. If a scourge made of bent nails has always caused me to spend my fuck liberally and quickly (not that speed is what I am most after), the pain and the damage are a thousand times that of the heather broom or knotted rope that the whores prefer ten to one—and who can blame them? In the case of the trollop previously evoked, I used a cat-o'-nines tied in a bundle and drew blood. Why, you ask, did I not employ the broom?

Like a riddle, my answer comes in threes. One: because I didn't think of it. Two: because she was a tough old bird with a bum like pedicle gneiss. And three: because (and here in a nutshell lies the crux of the matter) I had invented a remarkable Salve, which—and this I knew from previous experiments made upon my own flesh and which, if it amazes you and causes you no end of astonishment—*caused the wounds to heal within a day!* You see: I was a vicious bastard but no monster. I knew that a bum of satin was essential for a whore's *métier.* Further: When I was not laboring those bums, I was buttering the cunts of actresses. My buttocks, too, were manifest in the greater world. Thus the Salve! To demonstrate my good faith in these matters at least, the virtue of these *propos,* I offer you, estimable reader, my recipe. Here it is:


SADE'S SALVE

Take a good measure of beeswax of the best quality—that is to say, of a perfect whiteness, without insect parts or particles, of a fair translucence and pleasant odor. This is to be well mixed with almond oil until a soft paste is formed, at which point a jelly made with the seeds of red quinces, translucent and cooled, is to be stirred in little by little, until you have a substance of the consistency of— Ah! I find there is no known consistency that describes it! To this, add several drops of mallow essence, several drops of mauve, a touch of hyssop, a breath of *saponaire*. (The Salve's employment is to be preceded by a gentle washing of the irritated tissues in chicory water.)

The Salve will be valueless if the plants are not collected during very hot, very dry weather, and in the early morning. If the plants are damp, or collected in the heat of midday, or in the chill of the evening, the entire experience will waste the preparator's time. The Salve will be dead, cloying, sticky, and without translucence. June is the best time for chicory, July for mallow, et cetera, late August the only moment to gather quinces and so on—but this, everybody knows.

Again: The trollop's bum, as I have said, was as good as it had ever been—such is the exquisite efficacy of the Salve—better, in fact: For when I nearly stumbled over her in the street, she was, it must be said, the worse for wear. My ministrations included dinner—the best, she swore, she'd ever eaten—and a bath. It is true, as she claimed, that I whipped her, not in the name of the Virgin Mary, as the good friars do in the salty privacy of their holy fisheries, but in the name of goddess Ejacula. As to the use of knives—I am no butcher, nor am I feebleminded. Even an excellent Salve will not heal a puncture in a day—what would? But a rope burn? *Mais oui!* In the treatment of *those* tiger's stripes, I will vouch on my (threadbare) honor for my Salve's serviceability.

To return to the little whores of Marseille: I have always loved a fart. Not the ill-advised fart of a peasant born and bred on beans, but the judicious wind of a worldly strumpet fed on pasta and pomegranates, a zephyr seasoned with anise seed, sage, fennel, melissa, lavender, and coriander. My expertise in such matters enables me to tell you this: If at night a young lady is fed artichokes and chicory (Divine Chicory! I salute you!), a roasted onion bristling with cloves, a salad of dandelion, and an infusion of mint sweetened with honey, she will void generously and fragrantly the following morning a turd of such fragrance that Sainte Marguerite-Marie would have run from it weeping (delectating as she did only in the runny, stinking frass of diseased nuns). Then, if the wench breakfasts upon a nicely baked seedcake made of anise, fennel, and coriander, studded with candied angelica, by early afternoon her farts will provoke the envy of angels. And, in those susceptible to such tender pleasures, an erection to compete with a bull elephant's.

But wait! There is more! For if I do not say it, who will? Should you prefer to lap up the bile of toads, the cud of dying cows, the venom of Restif de La Bretonne, so be it! Poison yourself, for all I care! Impoverish your understanding. But I am not the devil that failed pornographer takes such pleasure in slandering! And if I am—or *was,* for now my soul yearns only for the smell of soup—partial to a perfumed fart now and then, barbarity I imagined only; foolishness, viciousness— to speak plainly—I indulged. I made a slave of no one; I never thrashed a whore I did not pay to thrash me; my closest accomplice was my wife. My antics were often ludicrous, rarely inspired—but I never hung a trollop by her feet, as Restif would have it (how appallingly vulgar is *that* imagination!).

Here, forthwith, the purpose of my miserable life: To banish imprecisions and banalities. To embrace the immense disorder of voluptuousness. To dare dwell in the marvelous territory of seduction. To articulate my active distrust of God and refuse His filthy impositions. To, in the limited time I have, with energy, vengefully and ragefully, dare uncover what God has hidden, dare illumine what man is forbidden to see.

# SEVEN

Sade, mon ami,

*How curious are mental forms! How they surge forth! Born of the mind, born of the heart, engendered by longing, by potent absences . . . My memory is not only a lens and a dream fan, it is also an aphrodisiac. Sade: I understand you better and better!*

*"There is no place for God in all my calculations,"* *Olympe once said to me. But then her lovely face grew pale and her eyes took on the crazed look of a trapped mammal. "I am attempting to perfect a machine to assure that I cannot be buried alive. Or, rather, that if it should it happen, despite all precautions taken, help will come within minutes and I shall be saved. For I cannot imagine—or, rather, I can only too well imagine—what it would be like to awaken in a coffin,*

*parched and terrified, cloaked in utter silence and pitch-darkness, barely able to move, and, what's worse, the earth in all directions pushing in, earth truffled with cadavers in all directions! And in every conceivable state of dissolution!*

*"I beg you to understand," she was quick to add, "I am not afraid of dying. Death is another thing entirely. I would die for the Revolution, if it would further the cause of Freedom."*

But for the fact that I am no longer ready to die for *the* Revolution, but only for *mine,* the description fits my mood exactly: parched and terrified. But here! I'll sing a little drinking song to remind myself that things could be worse. I'm not dead yet, after all, and there's not a corpse in sight. Although the asses complain and the grave digger's cart groans beneath the weight of the day's accumulation of crimes, heads and bodies both are trundled off, and the cobbles—I see them now, shining in the moon—are washed with water.

> *Pleasure is a delicate wine,*
> *Inebriate yourself one sip at a time.*

IN MONTMARTRE, THERE used to be a little inn called *Les Mystères*. Its walls were made of polished cherry. My favorite table was beneath the stairway, where I was served those simple but toothsome Parisian suppers with civility and grace by the owner himself. His name? Monsieur Mirebalais. His mustaches bristled, his dish towel flapped with each gesture of his hand like a sail in the wind. I recall platters of oysters—the best in Paris—and an onion soup scalding hot beneath its weeping crust of cheese. I recall a door opening on the landing above me, the sound of an irresistible laugh, and a girl named Lélise stepping lightly down the stairs in a scarlet jacket.

"Lélise, you are the Queen of Sheba!" I tell her as she passes. She gives me a kiss. Then, her guitar balanced on her opulent bosom, she sings with a dizzying effrontery (and the words belong to Voltaire):

> *He who fears the night*
> *Is not worthy of delight.*

But wait! Here is Madame Mirebalais with a dish of her celebrated medallions of eel served on croutons of bread fried in Isigny butter! And here is Lélise again, standing there before me, as beautiful as if she had surged forth from the sea of my most tempestuous dreams! She sings a poem of the *abbé* Courtin's that she has herself put to music:

> *To so much grace!*
> *To these, her tempting arts!*
> *To the beauty*
> *That strikes my heart!*

Lélise! Olympe! Gabrielle, my dearest: I raise my glass to you and say: "To so much grace!"

Now Madame's dinner continues; I am served duckling as shiny as a new copper pot and nesting in savory peas.

> *An exile*
> *In the gardens of bliss,*
> *I recognize Venus*
> *By her kiss!*

We have been exiled, dear creatures, *hélas.* And not in the gardens of love, twice *hélas, hélas!* But in the prisons of the Revolution, Our Revolution, and in Death.

Lélise has a prodigious *répertoire;* she sings the ancient ballads of Provence and the songs of old Paris, marvelous songs that one day no one will sing. As midnight approaches, she sings the songs of the Revolution:

> *We are the women of St-Denis;*
> *of La Hallen, of St-Antoine;*
> *We are ten thousand insurgents—*
> *Long live Liberty!*

And everyone in the room joins in the refrain:

> *Vive la Liberté!*

What Lélise sings is the truth: Ten thousand women had confronted the king and, in so doing, changed the face of France. Ten thousand strong, and Olympe and Gabrielle were among them.

The day of her arrest, Gabrielle had just completed a new series of fans. Freshly glued and open, they were laid out on the table to dry: the Games of Children—hoops and kites and skipping ropes, castles in the sand, kisses in the ring, knuckle-bones. . . .

*How I should love to wander the streets of Paris with a new fan and a dove-gray dress; to wander in the light of full spring, without the fear of treading in blood! Once the blood of cattle puddled the streets of the Rue des Boucheries; now every street in Paris deserves to be so named. Butchers' street: Marat lived there in hiding for a while. Marat, who was himself a butcher, stabbed in the heart by a new butcher's knife!*

*I have been told that when Louis was confronted in his palace by the crowd, a butcher's apprentice coiffed him with the red bonnet of the Revolution and made him drink to the Nation's health from a bottle of cheap red wine. That day a butcher informed the king that he was lost, as the people filled the palace like cattle and clung to the windows like flies.*

*It is dawning! Through the bars high above me I can see that it is snowing. May life be more generous to you, Sade, than it was to our foolish king. And your death more noble than his, more noble than my lost love's; more noble than mine.*

Ton amie,
*Gabrielle*

EIGHT

Several years ago, Gabrielle brought me Sahagún's *General History of the Things of New Spain*. These volumes she had procured after much effort from my family—they had once belonged to my uncle and were part of his marvelous library, most of it now destroyed. The friar's books have been of great service in our joint undertaking, our own brief reverie on the "Things of New Spain."

This morning my eyes were less painful—how the body atomizes in confinement!—and I was able to read again. I was struck by a fragment from Book Six—the book devoted to Moral Philosophy. These are the words spoken by an elder to a new ruler:

"O master, O ruler, O precious person, O valued one, O precious green stone . . . *Pay special attention*. Esteem thyself . . . Do not become as a wild beast, do not completely bare thy teeth, thy claws."

As he spoke, the elder wept. Perhaps because he knew how power corrupts. Perhaps the new ruler had already bared his teeth.

And now, as the day draws to an end, the Revolution, in a convulsion of self-disgust, cuts off the head of one whose teeth and claws have not ceased, these many years, to worry Liberty's throat with such hunger that even Robespierre feared for his life: I am speaking of the madman Hébert. His execution was impossible to ignore—Hébert bellowed and squealed like a gutted pig—and the crowd (and Restif was there, too, standing far off to the side), who had a week ago applauded him as he leapt over a basket heaped with heads, now roared with laughter to see him so flagrantly unmanned. Even Sanson quickened to their mood and made the blade dance above the naked neck before letting it drop with the sound of thunder and ice.

Before he was silenced, Hébert screamed louder than any-one—even the comtesse du Barry, whose cries had pierced my heart with grief. (Poor creature! Cut down for having fucked a king!) They tell me all the Hébertistes will loose their heads today; the crowd is the biggest yet, the tower trembles with the people's roars, and each time the blade comes crashing down I think I shall go mad. I attempt to write, cannot, put down the pen, pace, turn around and around my chamber pot like a Brahmin circumambulating a sacred shrubbery.

Hébert today, Robespierre tomorrow or the day after. Like Sir Hugonin de Guisay, he will be undone by his own game. Ah—but perhaps you do not know Sir Hugonin's exemplary story? Here it is then: He was a beast—vigorous, lusty, and of unprecedented temper. He liked to force the peasants in his path to crawl about on all fours, barking. One night, during Carnival, he painted himself with tar and rolled in black fleece to play the dancing bear for the king's amusement. The disguise was perfect—Sir Hugonin was unrecognizable. A servant approached with a torch and, peering into his face, cried: "Speak, bear! In the name of the king! Tell us who you are!" The fleece and the tar caught fire, and in an instant the dancing bear was transformed into a human torch. Thus will the beast, Robespierre, be undone.

GOD'S BALLS! HOW they carry on! Once the Revolution has gorged on the citizens of France and returned to her den to sleep for a century or two, what will happen to the triumvirate she whelped: Liberty, Equality, Fraternity—that vast heresy! That near impossibility! That acute necessity! Will they, her tiger cubs, continue to quicken the long night of our ignorance? Will their bright eyes illumine the interminable Dark Ages of Man?

HERE IS WHAT I wonder on my worst days: If the guillotine exemplifies Nature—perpetual, blind, deadly, inescapable—

and if Man is Her servant, and the Revolution too, then there is no hope. Then would I, and gladly, see the universe perish.

IN ORDER TO punish me for my rages (and I ask you: What caged animal does not succumb to rage from time to time?), my books, manuscripts, pens, and paper have been taken from me. Without them, I am lost. What is worse, I do not know if they will ever be returned.

Alone in my tower, disarmed, unmoored by pen and paper, my thoughts come unfixed (ink and fuck have always been the glue that holds my mind together); like the eggs of eels, my thoughts are dispersed by tides over which I have no control. In this state of rootless imagining, my mind seizes upon the most unexpected associations. Drops of fat suspended in my soup become the ocular devices of archons; a baneful spider stalking fleas exemplifies the pubic triangles of embalmed houris; a copple-crown turd warns of the Revolution's collapse and the dawning of lethal systems of industry. Further, to conjure anxiety I pretend that the lines of my palms are the river systems of dead planets; when that proves tedious, I examine the frayed threads of my sleeves. These suggest astrological signs indicating the day, month, and year of my release. Days pass, and the more I grapple with despair, the more stupefying are the systems I invent. To tell the truth, they are more irritating than entertaining! But then comes the thought that saves me from the perils of this insalubrious necromancy: I will dream a book!

## THE BOOK

Almost at once I imagine a large book bound in red leather, its gilded title stamped deeply into the cover and spine. I recall how once with Gabrielle I had visited the workshops in the Latin Quarter, where wenches of all ages—and many of them were wonderfully fuckable—folded, stitched, and bound the printed sheets and, if the book was *very* fine, passed the edges through gold.

I hand-print the sheets of my book, and so carefully do I reconstruct the process in my mind that I can smell the fresh ink as I lift each sheet from the press, and see the light of my mind's eye there where the metal letters have pressed into the paper, sensuous indentations like the mark of a finger in damp sand. One by one I set them out to dry, and then, luxuriating, I fold the sheets by hand, feeling the paper bend like a body beneath my hands. When all the pages are thus prepared, I set them in a sewing frame and, as I saw the women do, sew them together with thick, strong thread. When this work is completed—and it takes me an entire day—I hold the book securely in a vise and with a brass hammer round the spine. This hammering I do lovingly, taking an entire morning, the book giving way little by little beneath my ministrations.

Next I make the cover; the boards of ebony are sheathed with fine leather, the title and decorations applied with delicate metal tools that I have heated with care beside the fire.

Finally the book is glued to its cover, placed in a press, let to dry.

After a restless night, I open it. The marbled endpapers are green and gold; they evoke the luxuriant forests of the Yucatán. The next few pages—of thick paper, stiff and creamy beneath the touch—are blank. But then comes the frontispiece: a little Maya tiger, her speech in suspension before her face like a materialization of the wind. And I see for the first time that my dreamed book is our book, Gabrielle—the one we are writing together, you and I. It seems the moment has come for me to complete it. And if I cannot take up my notes to study, nor paper and pen, I can, nonetheless, engage a reverie. What are books but tangible dreams? What is reading if it is not dreaming? The best books cause us to dream; the rest are not worth reading.

~~~

# NINE

## THE TOPHET

*The miraculous text had dissolved, blanketing Landa's chamber in an acute malediction. Two friars were called in to carry the corpse from the room.*

*After the fish was buried and blessed, the remains of the scribe Kukum were tossed on a pyre. Soon after, Kukum's widow was sent away by the soldiers. They told her there was no need for her to return: Her flowers, the fragrant tixzula, had been fed to the Inquisitor's pigs, and her husband's body fed to the fire. Looking up at the sky, she saw smoke through her tears and knew they were speaking the truth.*

*For a time she gazed at the sky and then at the church, which was the color of a sick person's urine. Inside, the Mother of God—who wore a wheel on her head—was said to weep ceaselessly for the Maya, although the pope had sent word that Landa must find a way to make her stop. Her Son was in there, too, with a wheel on his head—just like the wheels of the carriages that sometimes crushed Indians to death; just like the wheels of the Inquisition, which broke bones and caused people whose common sense she had always respected to say crazy things without foundation in truth. As when Baltasar Puc said he had crucified a boy and a rooster and had with a knife cut out their hearts. With the same knife he had cut a cross into these hearts before offering them to the Old Gods, who were very angry but who refused to die. Everyone knew that the wheel had forced these lies from Baltasar Puc's throat, and other lies more terrible, besides. Later it was said that the day the body of the scribe Kukum was set aflame, the Mother of God wept pearls of black blood. Kukum's widow turned away from the friary gate weeping black blood, too.*

*From a high window, Melchor looked down and with a wildly beating heart stared at the sorceress who had bewitched him. He imagined her hanging by her breasts—a thing that caused many to repent.*

EARLIER THAT WEEK, *a small stash of idols had been found in a cave just outside Mani, and Landa had arrested a large number of Indians who, having been savagely whipped, admitted that more idols—countless numbers, in fact (and, miraculously, their numbers multiplied by the minute)—were hidden away in the mountains. The friars and the constables had scoured the entire territory for days, making hundreds of arrests and flogging everyone they could, pouring burning wax or molten lead into their wounds, lashing them to wheels to be broken, forcing filthy water down their throats until the blood flowed from their ears and they drowned.*

*The Indians described fantastic rituals; these confessions justified more arrests. Idols accumulated—some so ancient and weather-worn as to be barely idols at all, others surprisingly fresh-looking, clumsily carved: hideous things too ugly, even, for doorstops. Some were wonderfully beautiful, carved of jade or serpentine, cinnabar clinging to their etched surfaces like old blood. These things were dumped on the cobbles of the friary, at the feet of an exulting Landa.*

*One evening, when the friars had found an ancient stone altar carved in the form of a thickly coiled snake and covered from head to tail in feathers, an old woman—one who had survived the plagues, a woman whose face had been so often branded with fire it looked like a page from a book—rushed at the friars and their constables shouting. In an instant, and before anyone had seen it happen, the soldier's dogs were upon her and she had vanished beneath their paws and faces in a cloud of dust.*

*Night after night, after the cries of the tortured had stilled, Landa examined the things he was so eager to destroy. The most curious were very old sculptures of human monstrosities: hunchbacks forced to their knees by the weight of humps rising*

like hills from their backs, dwarfs barely able to stand on with-
ered legs, idiots grinning with cleft palates, a howling infant
metamorphosing into a jaguar, a truly satanic figure with a
snout and hooves. But one of these pieces was of particular
interest to Landa; carved of copey wood and fragrant with
copal, it showed two men embracing. For many long hours he
looked at the thing with fascination, recalling Aristotle: To
understand a thing is to suffer. *Landa suffered because he
understood the danger he was in. It took all his strength to
keep from caressing the wood with his fingers, from pressing it
to his burning cheek. Later, when he would be closely ques-
tioned in Spain, he would explain that the idols and other
objects he had reduced to rubble had been alive with an irresistible vitality, capable of contaminating the staunchest hearts.
To examine them was to come dangerously close to losing the
eternal struggle that frets so ceaselessly the human soul.*

AS MELCHOR CONTINUED to gaze out his window, the
day's second marvel occurred. As the sky thickened to night,
friars, soldiers and constables, and a crowd of people approached
the friary with what appeared to be . . . Yes! A great quantity of books! The blue books of the Maya, books fragrant with
incense, books Kukum had guarded with his life; books with
pages white with lime; books swarming with glyphs and stars
and numbers: the Maya's sacred library of black mirror days,
days of smoke, of vanished moons; days of sun, of ocelots and

*fish; days of eyes, days of dreams: poetic days, priceless, tragic, baneful days. Red and black, they tumbled and spilled across the cobbles; they glowed like live coals, causing the eyes of those who look upon them to water and burn.*

*The next day, and surely to quiet his anger, Landa was given a statue of the Virgin made of a paste of cornstalks and the roots of wild orchids. He complained the thing looked like a satanic pastry, fit for a witches' sabbath. The Virgin had crossed eyes and a sluttish smile. But the Indian who had made her was known to be devout, and so the Virgin was placed in the chapel—already cluttered with such gifts, including a Christ made of the same dubious materials, a figure Landa feared was meant to convey intense rage against the Church. The Christ's black lips curled back from teeth shattered by the violence of his agony, and a gnawed and ragged tongue. Worse: The Savior's back was so violently arched it was clear He wished to tear Himself from the Sacred Cross! What could this mean if not that the Son of God did not wish to submit to God's Will? But Landa did not chew on this for long; the Tophet was scheduled for the following week, and the friary needed to be made ready. The fountain and corridors were all draped in black cloth; a scaffold had been built—platforms, too; and shirts for the damned cut, dyed, and sewn.*

*That week, Melchor was plagued by a recurrent dream: He had been running in terror for a long time and, exhausted, sat down upon the roots of an old tree. He had been running because Mani was on fire, a fire so hot that buildings exploded with a sound like thunder and the bodies of people, Spanish and Indian alike, were thrown up into the air. As they were hurled across the sky by the force of the explosion, they grew wings or, like witches, straddled brooms. The fire caused a terrific wind, and all about him the air was filled with domestic animals, crockery, and blankets. Melchor realized with horror that what remained of Mani was now airborne: forks and spoons and pots of beans, boots and stools and frying pans.*

*Suddenly he was surrounded by strange figures: dwarfs and sows in dresses, and witches showing their breasts or lifting their skirts to fart black smoke and blue butterflies in his face. And then he saw what all the commotion was about: Kukum's widow, dressed not in her little white shift embroidered with flowers, but in a gown of scarlet silk and approaching swiftly with a retinue of giant hares.*

LANDA'S PUBLIC BURNING *was preceded by a parade: first, a flock of chanting friars carrying black flags and crosses swathed in black raised above them like standards; then the schoolchildren, their eyes to the ground and singing in voices hesitant and hollow; last of all, a throng of Indians so disfigured by torture their own children could not recognize them. Some wore stiff yellow shirts marked with red crosses; others were dressed in blood-soaked paper. A number had been so*

badly beaten the tendons and muscles of their backs had rup-
tured. Shaking, they walked bent in two, their hands, twisted
into claws, hanging at their sides.

Landa, flanked by four judges and his principal lieu-
tenants, stood on a high platform and bowed to the Spanish
dignitaries, secular and regular clergy, lesser officials, and indi-
vidual colonists who had come from as far away as Mérida,
Izamal, Valladolid. A crowd of Indians stood apart, held back
by soldiers and their dogs, which in their excitement howled
and barked ceaselessly, submerging the sobs and cries that
filled the air with a palpable throbbing. The faggots were prepared, the prisoners bound, hanged by their hands, and lashed
for the last time.

Landa unfolded a large piece of parchment embellished
with the watermark of the Inquisition: the cross, the sword,
and the palm branch. In a voice hoarse with ranting, so that he
sounded more like a raven than a man, he cried:

"I, Reverend Father Fray Diego de Landa, First
Provincial, Apostolic Inquisitor Against Heresy, Humors, and
Emptiness of Mind, Charms, False Opinions, Tittle-Tattle,
and Evil Effects; Sorcery in All Its Three Thousand Forms,
Vexations, Infections, Befoulment, and Unlucky Things;
Subtlety of Nature; Satyrs and Fauns; and by Virtue of His
Holiness's Bulls, and Apostasy in His Majesty's Dominions
of the Province of Yucatán, New Spain; having appointed a fit
house for the Audience and prisons and torture chambers of
the Holy Office, make it known to all assembled here today,

*July the eleventh, in the year 1562 of the Incarnation of the Redeemer:*

• *That these Indians—nobles, lords, and peasants— beneath the lashes and iron of the Holy Inquisition, have admitted to Witchcraft, evoking a demon named "Angel of Light"*

• *Have offered prayers to skulls and idols smeared with the blood of their bodies*

• *Have taken itinerant sorcerers into their homes and fed them and also kept hidden for them their bundles of necromantic tools*

• *Have ridden on horseback or on occasion worn forbidden things such as gold, silver, silk, coral, and pearls*

• *That they have manufactured and sold in the market of Mani obscene snuffboxes, indecent crosses, and the like*

• *Have painted their bodies with the stripes of tigers and, drawing blood from their ears, cursed God*

• *Have crucified small children, cut out their hearts, roasted them, and fed them to their idols—crimes so terrible they were acknowledged only after the most rigorous investigation*

• *Finally: They have hidden their blasphemous books and lied about them and continue to revere them and hold them precious above all things*

The prisoners, little more than meat, were bound and heaved into the fire, now raging. So great was the Tophet it *eclipsed the sun and for a time became the lamp of the universe. Landa, too, outshone the sun. Beneath him, the last of his enemies, the last Lords of Mani, the last heretics, librarians, and sorcerers, writhed and wormed their way into Hell.*

*Gloatingly, Landa recalled the subversive lispings of Copernicus, who in his folly believed in the sun's preeminence; Landa's Tophet was proof of the world's centrality.*

*"So much for the 'allegorical fires' of the so-called philosophers!" Landa shouted to Melchor above the fire, the dog's howlings, the screams of the damned. "My Tophet is the mirror of Hell, and it is God in His Infinite Glory who holds up that mirror today!" With a small gesture of his hand, Landa indicated that the sacred books, heaped together, should be fed to the fire. A column of smoke flooded the sky—it was so black, so thick, that Landa was certain God was watching. So great was the stench of burning flesh, of deerskin curling up like fingers, that surely God smelled the Tophet, too. And the cries of the damned. Surely He was listening.* What these people were, *Landa whispered,* I alone will say.

*LATE THAT NIGHT, the sky tore open from the west to the east with such violence the walls of the friary shuddered and the belfry bell rang out. Prostrate with heat, Landa gazed toward the window in time to see a horizontal bar of lightning ignite the sky. For a moment the sky was sliced into two distinct portions: the top a muddy green, the bottom the color and consistency of curdled cream. It began to rain.* If a flood should scour this land to the bone, that would be an act of Grace, *Landa thought,* and an act of Compassion.

*The Inquisitor rolled over. So damp was his bed, in such disarray, and, to tell the truth, so smelly, it seemed like the nest of some lesser mammal. Landa did not approve of baths—a thing the Indians in their vanity and lechery were so addicted to that, despite fines and lashings, they continued to indulge in. As Landa lay in his own familiar stench, the rain fingered his mind. He sank into a dream as into silt. Dreaming, he saw a woman fucked by a goat right in the public square of Mani, and no one seemed to care. The woman and the goat were going at it eagerly; the woman was holding the goat by its horns, straddling him while he sat like a king on a dazzling throne, his balls like great velvet cushions.*

*"Does no one care?" Landa shouted to the crowd of Indians and friars who walked hither and thither occupied by banalities. "Am I the only one to see?"*

IN THE MOST *secret of places, a place known only to her, in the deepest of caves far beneath Mani, in a circular room built within a natural declivity of red stones and turtle-egg mortar, Kukum's widow sits on the floor beside a candle, her husband's inkpot, and his bundle of uncut pens. Twelve of her people's most sacred books are here, wrapped in jaguar skin and buried in sand.*

*She burns incense to her husband's special gods: Itzamná—the god of writing—and old, old Pawahtún. And she burns incense to the god of corn. For are not books like bread? Do they not nourish our spirits just as corn feeds our bodies?*

*It comforts her to know the books are near. She has some berries with her; these she eats slowly, one by one, because they are bitter. Then she lies down to die.*

# TEN

Today my papers were returned to me, among them Gabrielle's last letter, which I had sorely missed. Here is a piece of it that I neglected to share with you before, gentle reader; I wish to do so now:

> . . . *The lessons began. If Olympe dictated with vivacity and eloquence, she was still prey to hyperbole, extravagant flourishes of speech that I, with care, attempted to tame. Her spelling was at best fantastical; she added letters to words she considered important. Or they were capitalized—a fault, you will agree, common to our age. To press a point she'd underline with such male energy she'd tear her paper.*
>
> *The lessons took place in my rooms above the* atelier, *rooms recently transformed by some extravagant gifts from the*

*Meanderer. A marvelous carpet of camel wool dyed with indigo and madder ignited the floor like a* feu de joie.

One afternoon, Olympe said: *"Would you, dear friend, take a dictation? For my head has been swarming with ideas ever since this morning, when I awoke having dreamed of a city unlike any the world has known, and yet it was Paris, Paris after the Revolution, perhaps.*

*"There were no famished crowds clamoring for bread, no lice-infested corpses lying in the streets. Glittering in the sunlight of full summer and studded with gardens, the city flourished within a ring of meadows—and beyond, a sprawl of Untouched Wildness many times larger than the city itself. These assured every quarter was perfumed by breezes (we underestimate the importance of the nose!). The city air smelled of pine needles, pollen, blossoms, rotting leaves. With the wilderness so near, the public gardens—buzzing with citizens planting rows of lettuce, seeding lupine, and poling beans—were bright with butterflies and birds. Deer grazed the parks, and pheasant roosted under the eaves.*

*"In times of Calamity—Famine, Plague, and War—the forests assured that a family, a group, or even the entire population could return to a State of Nature. Also, the wilderness, scattered with lakes and ponds, supplied the market year-round with trout and pike and eels.*

*"Every city square was planted with an orchard. The citizens came together in the fall to harvest hazelnuts, almonds,*

apples, and, in summer, cherries. Imagine an entire quarter planted with cherries! Every child with cherries dangling from her ears! Imagine the joy of children growing up in 'the Almond Quarter,' the pleasures of a city park shaded by one hundred walnut trees.

"At every crossroads, a fountain. The sound of water (we underestimate the importance of the ear!) lulling infants to sleep. A swamp," she added, dreamily, "at a certain distance, several days' journey perhaps, but well worth it because of the ibis nesting there."

"Is there a slaughterhouse in your dream city?" I teased her.

"If there is"—she smiled, indulging me—"its great portal is in the shape of a gaping mouth to remind all those who enter there that they, too, will be eaten in the end."

But this was not all. Her forest was "scattered with philosophers tending to matters of morality." In times of crisis, a citizen might wend her way through the trees to a "philosophical tower" and there discuss matters of the mind and heart. These towers were provided with observatories "so that anyone may take a long look at her origins and be inspired, be amazed.

"I imagine the citizens of such a city intellectually and morally autonomous," she said, "their talents and capacities multiple, as unwilling to be slaves as to see their children enslaved. I imagine such citizens knowledgeable in Law,

Medicine, Philosophy, the Sciences, and the Arts, and so assured of their own well-being. I imagine them standing tall as trees."

"There is one thing to be said for our city as it is," I said, putting down my pen. Rising, I took the combs from Olympe's hair one by one. "And it is that women have—and this for several generations, from the spirited marquise de Rambouillet to the exemplary atheist Madame du Deffand— opened their homes for debate. Yet it is extraordinary that after so much talk—of aesthetics, of politics, of ethics and morality—Parisians continue to rail at one another when they are not tearing out one another's throats! Marat, for one, would have us butcher our enemies and eat the flesh raw!"

"Madame du Deffand would not have invited him to supper twice!"

"If everyone smelled as good as you do," I said, planting a kiss on the crown of her head, "there would be no enmity among men."

"I fear that is not so," she sighed, "for I continue to cause a great deal of enmity." After a moment's reflection she added, "I've often wondered if Morality is an attribute of Reason. Of course, evil is always buttressed by 'reasonable' arguments. Yet, what if True Reason is an attribute of Morality, and True Morality an attribute of Reason?"

"You are imagining a New Morality," I said. "One that remains to be invented."

*"Exactly." Her smile was tender. "And this is why I dreamed a philosopher at the ready in each isolated tower, so that a citizen might contemplate Nature throughout the day and at night discuss Her virtues with a friend."*

*Olympe's lessons were punctuated by much laughter, cups of chocolate, and readings from Voltaire:*

We owe the theater to Shakespeare. Puissant and fecund, his genius was also artless and sublime, without an atom of good taste, without the least understanding of the rules.

*"It gives me hope!" Olympe exclaimed. "For I, too, have not an atom of good taste; I, too, know nothing of the rules."*

*She would always be a fanciful speller. She imagined that spelling was like pastry-making; one added flavors, raisins, and nuts at will. And how delicious beneath the tongue the phrase* gold is malleable. *"It brings butter melting on a piece of toast to mind!"*

*We relished words of particular resonance or potency, recalling how when we were children they evoked worlds, mysterious and entire, just as Cook's 'Otahiti' caused us to yearn for his tale, to lean into it as one leans into a fragrant breeze.*

*"To read," I told her, "I confused with 'to reed.' That is to say, to float in a little boat with my father among the rushes. Now, as I sit beside you and gaze into this open book, I have*

*the mood of that day, its weather and sweetness before me. As the clouds sail past the sun, the water changes color. And now, as you read the title of this book aloud, dear Olympe—"*

"To the Austral Pole and Around the World."

*"—my reverie deepens. Boat, sky, and water dissolve and give way to distant times, and places I have never seen but where I would travel gladly, if sometimes with sadness."*